Running Wild

Deputy Sheriff Cole Paston does not know what lies behind the trouble festering around Clear Spring, Kansas. He suspects Floyd Kennedy, the wilful son of Buck Kennedy the biggest rancher in the country, of being the cause of it.

Floyd was sent to prison for three years for trying to kill Mart, Cole's brother, after Mart had shot and wounded hotel owner Frank Bartram. To complicate matters further, Buck Kennedy is trying to take over the Paston ranch for Floyd, who is about to be let out of prison. Cole senses that the trouble is far from over, and he is right. When all hell breaks loose, bloodshed and murder rages until the last shot.

Running Wild

Corba Sunman

A Black Horse Western

ROBERT HALE · LONDON

ISBN 978-0-7090-9235-3

Robert Hale Limited
Clerkenwell House
Clerkenwell Green
London EC1R 0HT

www.halebooks.com

Typeset by
Derek Doyle & Associates, Shaw Heath
Printed and bound in Great Britain by
CPI Antony Rowe, Chippenham and Eastbourne

ONE

Cole Paston reined in his big chestnut on the ridge over-looking the Lazy P cattle ranch in Bolton County, Kansas, and stepped down from the saddle. He trailed the reins and walked a few steps, shrugging his wide shoulders and flexing his muscles as the rowels of his spurs tinkled musi-cally. It was a long twelve-mile ride from the nearby town of Squaw Creek, and he always pushed the chestnut hard when heading for home range. He sighed in relief as he looked down at the buildings of the ranch, and then cuffed the brim of his black Stetson back off his forehead. He clenched his hands into raw-boned fists when he caught sight of a moving figure in the doorway of the barn back of the ranch house and recognized his brother Mart. For the thousandth time in the last three years he won-dered what had happened in town the night Mart shot Frank Bartram, the local hotel owner. Mart never spoke about that incident although it transpired that he had acted in self-defence, and Bartram had never made a state-ment regarding the incident.

A spurt of emotion lanced through Cole's chest and

hardened his tanned features until his brown eyes looked like bottomless pits. His lips pulled tight against his teeth and his nostrils flared as he drew a sharp breath and sucked good Kansas air into his lungs. He watched Mart as his brother strode across the back yard to the rear of the house before turning back to his horse and swinging into the saddle. Sunlight glinted on the deputy sheriff star pinned to his blue shirt. He slipped his feet into the stirrups and reached instinctively for his .45 in its leather holster to check it was still snug and ready for use.

The chestnut moved forward instantly, heading down the slope for the cluster of ranch buildings. Cole straightened his shoulders and glanced around instinctively. Twenty-six years old, he was tall in the saddle, with big muscles rippling under his tanned skin. He had worked for the county law for three years now, since the trouble involving Mart had arisen, and, although the storm seemed to have blown over, Cole was aware that it was not finished, for Floyd Kennedy was getting out of prison any day now, and Mart had sworn to kill Floyd on sight; his reason, like the shooting of Frank Bartram, remaining secret. Kennedy had been sent to jail for attempting to shoot Mart.

Cole glanced around again when he reached the front yard, and his eyes narrowed to mere slits when he spotted two riders coming down the ridge to the left of the house. He recognized the big white stallion that Buck Kennedy always rode – a big, half-wild horse that was as vicious as its bullying master. Buck Kennedy, father of Floyd, owned the sprawling BK ranch to the north and west, but acted as if the whole of Kansas belonged to him.

The sound of the chestnut's hoofs in the still afternoon air brought Mart to the porch. He gazed at Cole, his bronzed face showing a tight grin. They were alike as two peas in a pod although Cole was four years older than his brother. Mart nodded a greeting. Cole pointed to the approaching riders. Mart glanced over his shoulder, saw them, and reached inside the doorway to pick up a Winchester carbine. He jacked a brass shell into the breech of the long gun and held the weapon in his left hand, the barrel resting in the crook of his elbow.

'It looks like that showdown I've been expecting is about to start, and Floyd ain't home from prison yet,' commented Mart. 'Maybe it's a good thing you are here, Cole. I might need a witness.'

'I wish I knew what the hell this is all about.' Cole stepped down from his saddle and tied his reins around a porch post. 'When are you gonna confide in me, Mart? I've talked myself hoarse more than once these past three years trying to get you to spill the beans, but you've never said a word about what went on, and all I've got to say now is, don't leave the telling too late. Buck Kennedy plays for keeps, so bear that in mind.'

'I don't know much more than you do!' Mart grimaced as he walked to the end of the porch to confront the two riders. They were coming across the yard at a canter. Buck Kennedy was fifty, a huge man with a violent temperament to match his bulk. His ruddy face showed something of his nature in its deep lines. His chin jutted aggressively over a bull neck. His blue eyes were cold, like broken glass. He ran 3,000 head of cattle on his big spread, and guarded each one of them jealously. He had hanged horse-thieves and rustlers without recourse to the law, and had taken a horsewhip to Lance Gifford on the main street of Squaw Creek in front of half the town, including the sheriff, as punishment for an unintentional insult young Gifford had paid to Buck's daughter Jane, a twenty-year-old wildcat with a temper more fractious even than her father's.

Buck Kennedy reined in close to the porch. He had to use all of his considerable strength to hold in his stallion as the brute stretched its neck and attempted to savage Mart, who remained immobile but took care to stay out of reach of the animal's teeth. Buck looked Mart over as he might view a dead cougar caught in the act of attacking one of his steers. His hard gaze shifted to Cole before returning to Mart, and his expression tightened as he set his jaw.

'I want to talk to you,' Kennedy grated.

'You've got nothing to say that I'll wanta hear,' Mart responded belligerently. 'But say your piece and then get out.' He turned his gaze to Kennedy's foreman, Bill Mason, a tall, thin beanpole of a man. 'What the hell are you doing here, Mason? I warned you to stay off my grass, so turn around and get the hell out.'

'I brought him along,' Kennedy boomed angrily. 'Hold your horses.'

'I'll listen to you after he's gone and not before,' Mart replied obstinately. 'Get going, Mason, or you'll take a slug to help you on your way.'

Mason sneered and sat immobile in the saddle of his grey. Mart lowered his left arm until the muzzle of his carbine gaped at Mason's chest.

'You're looking through those pearly gates right now, Mason,' Mart warned in a harsh tone. 'Get moving or you'll pass through them so quick you won't get a chance to speak to Saint Peter. I ain't in the habit of grinding my coffee twice so rattle your hocks – and don't set foot on Lazy P range again.'

'OK,' said Kennedy heavily. 'Get out of here, Bill. Wait for me on the other side of the stream back there.'

Mason turned his horse and rode back across the yard. Mart watched him, his pale eyes unblinking. Cole heaved a sigh and shook his head. He felt out of his depth in this situation, and feared it would get out of hand. He watched Kennedy fighting to control his horse, and wondered what made the man tick. Buck Kennedy had just about every-thing in the world that any man could wish for, but he was not satisfied. His son and daughter, too, always acted as if they owned everything in sight. Floyd going to prison had brought a measure of peace to the county, but he was due home any time now.

'What brings you here?' Kennedy demanded, gazing at Cole.

'This is my home,' Cole replied. 'Where else would I be when I'm off duty?'

'It won't be your home much longer.' Kennedy hauled on his reins as the spirited stallion reared and flailed its forelegs dangerously close to Mart's head. 'I figure to buy you out, so name your price and I'll pay it. Floyd will be home any time now and I don't want trouble. I don't know what the hell happened three years ago, but I do know there will be no more of it.'

'You're wasting your time and your breath,' said Mart. 'Lazy P ain't for sale, and I wouldn't sell it to you even if I was planning on quitting, so if you've got nothing else to say then high-tail it.'

'I'm trying to do this right,' Kennedy grated, 'but you

sure make it hard for a man to be civil. I'm bending over backwards to keep this friendly. Name your price and you can ride out of here in one piece. I could send a dozen of my outfit in here to stamp you into the dust. After the trouble between you and Floyd I don't want you around. I've heard about the threats you've made against my boy, and I ain't gonna stand by and watch it happen. Name your price and we'll settle the deal. You can pull out and start up some place else.'

'I'm not going anywhere,' retorted Mart. 'Floyd broke the law so he's the one should stay away. I remember you hounding my father into his grave, trying to steal this place from him. But you didn't succeed then, and I'll see you in hell before I'll let you ride roughshod over me.'

Cole stepped forward to Mart's side and placed a hand on his brother's right arm.

'Take it easy,' he advised. He looked into Kennedy's tense face. 'You better ride out, Kennedy. You've said your piece. You know how Mart feels about selling. It ain't ever gonna happen. And I'll remember your threat, just in case. You'd better pull in your horns before I take you seriously and arrest you.'

'If you think that law star you're wearing scares me any then you're way out of line,' rasped Kennedy. 'It won't protect you when the chips go down.'

Cole shook his head. 'Beat it,' he said heatedly. 'It looks like you rode in on the prod. If you don't leave now I'll arrest you for disturbing the peace.'

Kennedy bared his teeth in a travesty of a grin. He pulled the head of his horse around and touched spurs to its flanks. The half-wild animal set off across the yard, jumping and bucking, arching its back, its head down as it left the ground in straight-legged leaps. Kennedy yelled, and the sound echoed across the yard. Cole watched the rancher intently, half-expecting him to reach for his holstered pistol. But at that moment a rifle cracked from across the stream beyond the corral and a slug passed between Cole and Mart to thud into the sun-warped boards of the house.

Mart lifted his Winchester to his shoulder and triggered three swift shots in reply. Cole drew his pistol, waiting for Kennedy to buy into the action, but the rancher, intent on getting clear of the yard, kept his back to the porch. Cole switched his attention to the stream. He saw gunsmoke drifting on the breeze, and spotted two riders sitting their mounts under a cottonwood. He recognized Bill Mason, saw gun smoke flaring around the BK foreman, and tilted the muzzle of his pistol for a distance shot, keenly aware that he and Mart had already been fired on.

The .45 recoiled against the heel of Cole's hand and the stink of burned powder filled his nostrils. Mason jumped as if someone had stabbed him with a knife, and then pitched sideways out of his saddle. Mart fired his Winchester again, and the second rider turned abruptly to seek cover beyond the fringe of trees along the far side of the stream.

'Who was the second man over there?' Cole demanded, and Mart shrugged.

'It looked like Buster Askew.' Mart looked around for Buck Kennedy, his features screwed into a grimace. 'It looks like the chips are down at last. It's been a long time building to an open fight.'

'I wish I knew what the hell it is all about,' Cole said sharply. 'You better keep to the house until I get back.'

11

'What are you gonna do?'

'Check out Bill Mason and arrest him if he ain't dead. Then I'll pick up that rider who was with Mason. After that I'll arrest Buck Kennedy. I reckon a spell in jail will cool him off.'

'I'll ride with you,' Mart said instantly.

'You'll do like I tell you and stay out of it,' Cole grated. 'This is law business. I'll handle it.'

Mart shrugged. 'Have it your way,' he rasped, 'but I think you're playing it wrong.'

'Wise me up to what happened three years ago and maybe I'll have a better understanding of the situation.' Cole looked into Mart's pale features and noted the hard glint in his brother's pale eyes.

Mart shook his head. 'It's my business, and you don't need to know,' he said.

'OK.' Cole nodded. 'If you keep your mouth shut you'll leave me no option but to play the cards as they fall, and read this game from my point of view.'

He crossed the porch and swung into his saddle. The chestnut headed across the yard and passed around the corral. Cole looked around for Buck Kennedy and saw the rancher in the distance, apparently heading back to BK – fighting his big stallion every step of the way. Cole looked ahead to the stream. Mason's horse was standing beside the inert body of its rider. There was no sign of the second rider.

The chestnut splashed through the hock-deep stream and lunged up the far bank. Cole reined in beside Mason. His gun was in his right hand and he looked again for the second man. When he was satisfied that he was alone he stepped down from his saddle and examined Mason. The

BK foreman was inert, his rifle discarded at his side. Cole grasped the foreman's shoulder and turned him over. Mason's sightless eyes stared up at him. A large stain of blood was seeping from the bullet wound in the centre of Mason's chest. Cole sighed and shook his head, still wondering what the trouble was all about.

He got to his feet and looked around. Hoofprints led under the cottonwoods and he followed them through the fringe of trees until he could see the undulating range beyond. He caught a glimpse of a rider ascending a slope a couple of hundred yards away to disappear over the crest almost instantly.

Cole restrained the impulse to take out after Kennedy, aware that he would be foolhardy to try and take on the BK outfit alone. It would be more sensible to take Mason's body to town and inform the sheriff of the turn of events. They had discussed the situation several times over the past weeks, trying to plan future action, certain that trouble would blossom the minute Floyd Kennedy came home from prison, and hoping to be able to nip it in the bud.

Cole loaded Mason face down across his saddle and led the horse back across the stream. He returned to the ranch and dismounted in front of the porch. Mart stood in the doorway of the house, Winchester ready in his hands. He gazed at Mason's body without emotion.

'You'd better saddle up and come with me to town,' said Cole. 'I want to bring the sheriff into this as soon as possible.'

'I'm not leaving the spread.' Mart shook his head. 'Kennedy is sure to be back, and he'll likely burn the place if he finds it deserted.'

13

'You're not gonna stay here. Don't argue, Mart. Saddle your horse and ride with me. Just do like I tell you. I don't need you making life any more difficult than it has to be.'

Mart looked into Cole's hard face. It seemed that he would dig in his heels, but he heaved a sigh and nodded reluctantly.

'OK,' he agreed grudgingly. 'But don't be surprised, when you come back this way again, if you find the spread burned down.'

'That would be better than coming back to find you trampled into the dust,' Cole responded grimly. 'Just grab what you might need and let's get out of here. I want to warn the sheriff that Kennedy is on the rampage at last. We've been expecting it.'

Mart went off to saddle his horse. Cole stood on the porch looking around, shocked by Buck Kennedy's behaviour. The silence was intense. There was no movement anywhere on the range. But he did not doubt that someone from the BK ranch was out there keeping watch. He looked at the motionless body of Bill Mason and shook his head in disbelief. For a long time he had reckoned that trouble would explode on the range when Floyd Kennedy came home from prison, but what had occurred took some understanding.

Mart came across the yard leading his roan. Cole tied the reins of Mason's horse to his saddle horn. He was in the act of swinging into his saddle when he caught the sound of rapidly approaching hoofs. He grabbed his pistol and stepped down into the dust again to ready himself for possible action.

'Rider coming in,' he said briefly.

Mart dragged his Winchester out of its saddle boot and

cocked the weapon. Cole walked to the left front corner of the house. He saw a rider coming around the barn, cocked his .45, and covered the newcomer, his expression hard, his dark eyes narrowed. When he recognized the newcomer he did not relax.

'It's Lance Gifford,' Cole observed, 'and he's riding as if his tail is on fire.'

'He probably rode into Buck Kennedy,' Mart mused. 'We ain't the only men in the county getting trouble from BK.'

Lance Gifford pulled his horse down to a walk as he crossed the yard. He lifted a hand in greeting when he saw Cole waiting for him.

'Say, am I glad to see you, Cole!' he called. 'I met Buck Kennedy on the trail north of here and he started shooting at me for no reason at all.'

'Simmer down, Lance,' Mart advised. 'Kennedy was in here on the warpath.'

Gifford stepped down from his saddle. He opened his mouth to speak and then caught sight of Bill Mason, face down across his saddle.

'Hey, that's Bill Mason you've got there! What happened?'

Cole looked around the yard while Mart explained the incident. Gifford, a tall, slim, fair-haired youngster aged twenty-two, shook his head in disbelief as he listened.

'I guessed Buck Kennedy would go off half-cocked when Floyd got out of prison,' he said, shaking his head, 'but I didn't think he'd start a shooting war.'

'Floyd ain't home yet,' Mart reminded.

'That's where you're wrong. My pa came back from Caribou Ridge last night – we don't use Squaw Creek after

Kennedy whipped me – and Pa said he saw Floyd there with a couple of hardcases. Floyd was raising a ruckus in the saloon and the local deputy was trying to quieten him down.'

'There's only one thing will cool off Floyd and that's a slug in the guts,' said Mart.

'Ride into town with us, Lance,' Cole invited. 'I want you to tell the sheriff about Kennedy cutting loose at you.'

'I was on my way in to town to see Sheriff Horden,' replied Gifford.

'Are you still seeing Hannah?' Mart demanded.

'Sure I am.' Gifford grimaced. 'She's never had any-thing to do with Floyd.'

'Tell that to Floyd.' Mart laughed harshly. 'He went to jail for trying to prove to me that she was his girl.'

'I didn't know that was the reason he pulled a gun on you,' observed Cole. 'But let's get moving, and you can tell me about it on the ride to town.'

'There's nothing more to tell.' Mart shook his head. 'I decided I didn't want any further trouble after I shot Bartram so I stayed away from Hannah. After the whip-ping you took from Buck Kennedy, Lance, I figured it was just plain cussedness the way you went after Hannah, knowing Floyd was interested in her. But maybe you like playing with dynamite.'

Gifford shook his head. 'I reckon as how Hannah is the only girl for me. I'm hoping to marry her next year,'

'I reckon Floyd will have something to say about that,' opined Cole as he led Mason's horse across the yard.

Gifford rode in beside Cole and Mart followed behind. They left the ranch and took the trail to Squaw Creek. As they ascended a ridge a rifle cracked somewhere to their rear. Gifford uttered a cry and fell forward over the neck of his horse. He dropped to the ground and lay crumpled in the dust. Mart twisted in his saddle, his rifle in his hands.

'There's gunsmoke over by that tree on the left,' Mart reported. He sent three quick shots in reply as Cole dismounted and bent over Lance. Cole heard the rattle of hoofs and looked up quickly to see Mart spurring his horse at a gallop across the range.

'Come back, Mart,' Cole yelled, but his brother ignored him.

Pausing just long enough to ascertain that Gifford was still alive, Cole regained his saddle, dropped the reins of Mason's horse, and set out in pursuit of Mart. He saw a rider appear briefly beside the tree Mart had indicated, heard another shot, and ducked as a slug crackled in his right ear. The ambusher turned his horse and rode out of sight. Mart continued to the tree and reined in. Cole joined him, and they watched a rider disappearing into a dry wash some 200 yards ahead. Mart threw up his rifle and took aim, but the rider vanished before he could fire.

Cole slid out of his saddle and looked for hoofprints. He found some, and examined them long and carefully before regaining his saddle.

'Is Lance OK?' asked Mart.

'The bullet hit him in the flesh of his left shoulder.' Cole swung his horse. 'We'd better push on. I expect a posse will come out before dark, and I want to ride with it.'

They returned to where Gifford was lying. The youngster was conscious but unmoving, and made no complaint when Cole bound up his wound with a neckerchief.

'Do you think you can ride on?' Cole asked.

'Just put me in my saddle and watch me,' Gifford replied stoically. 'Kennedy has overstepped the mark at last, and now we can go for him. My father will turn our crew out to fight, and Kennedy will get stomped for this. His days are numbered.'

'We don't need a range war,' said Mart. 'That's a game no one can win.'

Cole looked around as they continued. The range seemed deserted, but he sensed that hostile eyes were watching them, and prepared himself mentally for yet another attack. He scanned the surrounding ridges as they continued, and felt uneasy when nothing untoward happened.

They were some four miles from Squaw Creek when Mart suddenly reined in and pointed ahead.

'Looks like more trouble, Cole,' he observed.

Cole, who had been covertly watching their back trail, faced his front, and reached for his pistol when he saw five riders sitting their mounts across the trail ahead. Sunlight glinted on drawn weapons. He saw quick movement among the waiting riders, and the next instant the silence was shattered by the crackle of gunfire.

Mart dismounted quickly, his Winchester in his hands. He dropped into cover and began shooting fast, triggering his carbine in an angry reply. Cole drew his Colt. He could recognize one or two of the men confronting them, and knew that these were Buck Kennedy's top guns. Lance Gifford uttered a low cry, more of surprise than pain, and slid out of his saddle to lie motionless on the grass, his arms out flung and blood spurting from a bullet wound in his right hip.

Cole dropped to one knee and raised his pistol. He

emptied the weapon with a burst of rapid shooting, and was grimly satisfied to see two of the five men drop limply out of the fight.

TWO

Buck Kennedy spurred his big stallion out of gunshot range of Mart Paston's rifle and gained cover behind a crest. He angled north to cross the stream where he had told Bill Mason to wait, and reined in when he spotted Buster Askew riding out fast. He watched Cole canter out from the ranch to check Mason. Kennedy grimaced when he saw Mason being thrust face down across his saddle. He drew his pistol and raised it to cover Cole, but sunlight glinting on the law star pinned to Cole's shirt front made Kennedy hesitate. He holstered the pistol and rode north to make contact with Askew.

Kennedy's mind was filled with bleak thoughts. He had been waiting for his son Floyd to return home from prison before setting out to exact payment from all and sundry that had a hand in putting Floyd in jail, but his impatience had got the better of him, what with the way the Pastons were making progress with their spread. But more than that, he had become increasingly concerned by the rumours that had been growing about a bank robbery that had occurred some thirty years before. Having been involved in the robbery, in which a bank teller had been killed, Kennedy was afraid the truth of that long past robbery would come out.

He had reason to believe that Mart and Cole Paston were behind the talk of the robbery, and he was out to silence several men who could upset the apple cart. He was wary of killing Cole Paston because of the law star Paston was wearing; for although he had some influence over Pete Horden, the local sheriff, he was aware that he could not hope to get away with murdering a deputy. He had planned to buy out the Pastons, but Mart was obviously not of a mind to sell, so the brothers would have to be got rid of the hard way. He smiled when he thought of how he had killed their father, Mike Paston, and arranged his death to look like a hunting accident – Mike had been in on the bank robbery.

Kennedy was pleased to find Buster Askew waiting for him on the trail to the BK ranch as previously ordered, and grinned when he saw several of his outfit approaching from his ranch headquarters. He reined in, shaking his head. He had been hoping to get rid of the Pastons legally, but there were other ways of removing them, and now that he had started a clean-up he would not stop until it was all over.

'Mason is dead, boss.' Askew's fleshy face was grim. He was tall and powerfully built, with blue eyes and fair curly hair. He wore his pistol on his left hip, butt forward.

'Who killed him?' asked Kennedy.

'It was Cole Paston, and Mason fired the first shot.'

'There must be something wrong with your eyes,' responded Kennedy. 'I saw Mart Paston fire the first shot.'

'You couldn't see what happened from where you

were,' retorted Askew. He paused, and then nodded. 'Uhuh! I get your drift, boss. Mart Paston didn't give Mason a chance. He cut loose without warning. But you know the sheriff will take Cole Paston's word above yours, so how are you gonna swing it?'

'If Pete Horden wants to stay in his job as the sheriff then he'll do like he's told,' Kennedy declared. 'Leave him to me. Just remember what you've got to say.'

'OK, boss.' Askew grinned crookedly and moistened his lips.

'Take these men and get ahead of the Pastons,' Kennedy continued. 'They'll be heading to town now. I don't want them killed while Cole Paston is wearing a law star so I'm gonna ride into town to wise up the sheriff. He'll toe the line. Just remember what I've said. I don't want anyone killed until after I've spoken to Horden.'

'We won't be able to keep them clear of town for long if we can't kill 'em,' Askew protested.

'That's OK. Just follow my orders. When I've finished my business in town I'll ride out to find you, and then we'll kill them. Just make sure you're somewhere on the trail between Lazy P and town. You should be able to keep the Pastons busy until I get back '

Askew nodded and motioned to the riders. They set off along the trail to town. Kennedy watched them until they were lost to sight before touching spurs to his horse and sending the big animal across the range towards the distant town. He let the stallion have its head, and the pounding hoofs of the great horse quickly ate up the miles.

Squaw Creek appeared to rise up out of the range as Kennedy neared it – stark and unlovely, a huddled collec-

22

tion of nondescript, unpainted wooden buildings warping under the daily attention of the burning sun. There was only one street – a dust-bath in summer and a quagmire in bad weather – and it was bordered by places of business and the drab homes of the community.

Kennedy entered the street and rode to the sheriff's office. The town was quiet, with little movement along the broad thoroughfare. Here and there a loafer sat in the shade, but no one acknowledged his arrival, and Kennedy smiled as he considered that he was disliked or feared by everyone who knew him. But that was the way he liked it. He had settled on the BK ranch thirty years before, even before the town had been founded, and regarded everyone who had arrived after him as interlopers. He ruled his kingdom of grass with an iron hand, and had buried a number of men who tried to muscle in on the range.

He glanced at the bank as he passed by, and saw a tall blocky man, a stranger, emerging from within. Kennedy eased his pace for a second look. The man met his gaze, did a double-take, and then lifted a hand to beckon Kennedy, who reined in towards the sidewalk.

'You want me?' Kennedy demanded.

'I don't know you,' the man replied. He had cold blue eyes that seemed to bore a hole in Kennedy. 'But I was told Buck Kennedy rides a white horse – the only one in the county. I'm Len Porter. I've just got a job here as a bank guard. Mr Liffen asked me to look out for you, and to tell you he wants to talk to you real bad. Will you go in and see him now? I'll hold your horse.'

Kennedy grinned. 'I'd like to see what kind of a job you'd make trying to hold this devil,' he replied. 'I ain't got time right now to stop for Liffen. Tell him I'll look in later.'

'He won't like that,' Porter replied harshly. 'He said it was important.'

'So is my business in town.' Kennedy glanced around. 'Tell him he'll have to wait.'

He swung his horse away and continued along the street until he reined up at the hitch rail in front of the law office. He stepped down from his saddle, tied his reins to the rail, and sidestepped the stallion as it craned its neck in an attempt to bite him. The door of the office stood open. Kennedy paused on the boardwalk and glanced around once more, his right hand resting on the butt of his holstered pistol. He pulled the brim of his Stetson lower over his harsh gaze and looked for signs of trouble, but the town was silent. He moved lightly despite his bulk, and stepped into the dim interior of the office.

Pete Horden was seated at his desk toward the rear of the office. An alley window on the left was ajar and the slightest suspicion of a breeze twitched the papers littering the desk. The sheriff was a tall thin man in his early fifties. His rugged face bore a cynical expression. His mouth was a thin slit with lips that barely showed, for he had a habit of compressing them as if afraid that a smile might inadvertently reveal itself. His dark eyes held no glimmer of sentiment. He looked up and leaned back in his seat when Kennedy blocked out the sunlight in the doorway, but did not acknowledge the BK rancher's arrival. Kennedy strode to the desk and dropped into a chair beside it.

'I haven't seen you around lately, Buck,' Horden said at length. 'What's brought you out of your lair?'

'There's some trouble needs sorting before Floyd gets

back.' Kennedy thrust his hat back off his forehead to reveal a shock of short grey hair. 'I rode into Lazy P and made an offer to buy the spread but Mart Paston took it the wrong way. Bill Mason was with me. Paston was spoiling for a fight, I reckon, because he told Mason to beat it. Bill rode clear, and I pulled out when I saw that Paston was wound up. Then there was a shot, and I saw Bill fall dead.'

'The hell you say!' Horden leaned forward in his chair. 'Did you see Cole Paston at Lazy P? He left here a couple of hours ago to visit with his brother.'

'He was there.' Kennedy nodded. 'He didn't say a word. I reckon he'll come back here with a different story to mine, but you've got the rights of it, Pete. Mart Paston shot Bill Mason in cold blood. It was murder, and I got a witness. Buster Askew saw it happen and he'll make a statement to that effect when he shows up here.'

'So that's your story, huh?' Horden nodded slowly. 'Now you'd better tell me what really happened before I decide what to do. I told you to hang fire on that deal until after Floyd got home from prison. If you've muddied the water by going off half-cocked, then you've tied my hands and I won't be able to swing anything your way. I do have to stay inside the law, you know, or at least appear to.'

'All you've got to do is fire Cole Paston from his deputy job so he can be taken care of,' Kennedy said harshly. 'I can't kill him while he's wearing a badge. I told you three years ago it was bad judgement to take him on. Now I want him out of the way, but he's safe behind his badge.'

Horden shook his head and grimaced. 'Folks around here think a lot of Cole,' he mused. 'They won't stand for him getting the dirty end of the stick in any deal you come up with. Heck, he's a damn sight better lawman when he ain't trying than I am doing my damnedest, and folks around here know that only too well. Where is he at right now?'

'Askew and four of my crew are keeping him and Mart occupied on the range while I'm in here talking to you. What do you want I should do about him?'

Horden heaved a long sigh. His expression showed that he did not like what he was hearing. 'For God's sake don't let him get back here to make a report on what happened at the Lazy P,' he said at length. 'The less folks know the better. You'd better head on out of town again and make sure your outfit get both Pastons. Kill them and bury them some place where they won't be found. If you can do that then you'll still be in business. But if you make a hash of getting rid of them then you'll lose out. If they show up here with their version of what happened then you won't have a leg to stand on. No one is gonna believe you.'

Kennedy grimaced. 'You ain't being much help, Pete. Are you getting soft in your old age?'

'The hell I am! You better realize that times have changed, Buck. We wouldn't get away now with some of the capers we pulled thirty years ago. I'm walking a thin line these days, and you'd better wise up to the situation before you get in too deep.'

'I'm in over my head already,' Kennedy rasped. 'OK, if that's the way you wanta play your cards. I'll handle the deal your way and come back to you later.'

Kennedy arose and walked to the door. He paused and glanced over his shoulder at Horden, who met his gaze and shook his head slowly. 'Do you reckon we couldn't get away with another bank robbery like the one we pulled over at Mulejaw Bend thirty years ago, Pete?'

'I shouldn't wanta try it these days,' Horden responded. 'I've managed to live down the past, and that's the way it's got to stay. And talking of that bank robbery, you better know that Bob Liffen told me Frank Bartram is saying more than he should about that crooked deal. It looks like Bartram is going to pieces. I've seen him going downhill this past year. You better have a talk with him before he says something that will blow us all away.'

'The hell you say!' Buck Kennedy's expression tightened and his eyes took on a hard glint. 'What is getting into these men we rode with in the old days? Is it because they're getting old? I heard Mike Paston shooting off his mouth about what he knew, and how he wanted to atone for the wrong he did – that's why I killed him.'

'He shoulda known better.' Horden's eyes glinted. 'All that stuff is gone and forgotten. It can't do anyone any good to rake over those particular coals. I'd have killed Mike if I'd got to him first. But that ain't all of it, not by a long rope. Liffen has got himself a bank guard – real salty guy. When I saw Len Porter I went in and had a word with Liffen, and he sure looked scared about something. When I got it out of him he said he reckoned Frank Bartram was about to spill his guts about the Mulejaw Bend robbery.'

'I don't believe this!' Kennedy shook his head. 'What's got into Bartram? He was the one that killed the bank guard at Mulejaw, and if it comes out now about that job then he'll be the one who'll get a rope around his neck.'

'I talked to him, but Bartram ain't been in his right mind since Matt Paston beat him to the draw three years ago. Frank has been simmering about something ever since.'

'We've got to stamp hard on this before folks really start

27

asking questions,' Kennedy growled. He gazed at Horden for some moments, and then shook his head and departed.

He swung into his saddle and rode along the street at a canter, but reined up in front of the two-storey hotel when he heard his name called. His eyes narrowed when he saw Frank Bartram, sitting in his wheelchair in the hotel entrance. Bartram had been crippled by Mart Paston in their shoot-out three years before, and was confined to a wheelchair.

'What's doing on the range, Buck?' Bartram demanded when Kennedy dismounted and tied the stallion to a post. 'I ain't seen you in a coon's age. I was beginning to think you had deserted your old friends. Is Floyd home yet?'

'He's due any day,' Kennedy replied. 'And we'll be paying a few debts when he shows up. Some folks around here think they've got away with what happened three years ago, but I've got a long memory, Frank. The chips are going down in a new game. I've been waiting to start cleaning up on the range, and now the time is right. How are you keeping? Still got no feeling in your legs?'

'I've given up all hope of getting back on my feet.' Bartram was forty years old; had been in his prime when he tangled with Mart Paston. But now his pale face showed the pain he had suffered; his eyes revealed the inner torment he felt because he was no longer able to walk. He was a small man, and looked smaller in the wheelchair. Physical inactivity over the past three years had wasted his powerful body. His wife had left him after the shooting, and with her departure the sunshine had disappeared from his life. He had slipped into the depths of despair and no longer cared for himself.

28

'You never told anyone what happened between you and Mart Paston, Frank,' mused Kennedy. 'I heard tell there was a woman involved, and it wasn't your wife.'

'I don't talk about that, ever.' Bartram gripped the wheels of the chair until his knuckles showed white. 'But I'm ready for the day when I set eyes on Mart Paston again. He might think the business was settled when he shot me, but I'm biding my time. He hasn't been near or by me since it happened, but he'll make the mistake of coming within range one day, and then I'll put him down in the dust.'

'I always meant to ask you if you put Floyd up to tangling with Mart Paston. It seemed too much of a coincidence that Floyd had a go at Paston after you were shot.'

'I don't know why Floyd went for Paston.' Bartram shook his head. 'Whatever Floyd's reason, it had nothing to do with me. But knowing Floyd for what he is, I'm expecting him to resume his trouble with Paston the minute he returns. In fact I'm looking forward to that. If I can't get Paston then I hope Floyd will.'

'Floyd won't do that.' Kennedy shook his head. 'They'd send him straight back to prison if he ever pulled a gun again. I reckon he should be a whole lot smarter now. In any case, I'm handling the deal for him. I've just reported to Horden that Bill Mason was shot dead by Mart Paston earlier today. The law will take care of the Pastons and they'll no longer figure in the deal. I'll see you around, Frank. I've got things to do right now.'

'What the hell happened, Buck?' Bartram gripped the wheels of his chair and his face changed expression. He reached out a long arm and grasped Kennedy's left wrist

29

in a powerful grip. 'You'd better be careful what you're doing. I have bad dreams about the Mulejaw job coming out. It's haunted me for years. I was the one killed the bank teller, remember, and they'd hang me if someone dug out the facts.'

'Don't be a fool, Frank.' Kennedy broke free of Bartram's grasp. 'Get a grip on yourself. No one will ever get to the bottom of that job. It happened all of thirty years ago.'

'There's the four of us left who pulled the job! Horden won't want the truth to come out since he lived it down, and Liffen is sitting quietly in his bank, making a fortune lawfully these days. He doesn't need to rob a bank now he owns his own. You're the only one making ripples in the creek, Buck. Why don't you pull in your horns? I tried to kill Mart Paston three years ago because he said something that made me think his father told him about our bank job. I figured Mike had wised him up. We've all done well since that Mulejaw job, and we don't need it to come up again.'

Kennedy grinned. 'Don't worry. I'm watching points closely. That's why I killed Mike Paston. He was beginning to drink heavily, and talked about things that were best forgotten. He had to be put down before he spilled the beans.'

'You killed Mike! Heck, I didn't think his death was accidental! Does the sheriff know about that?'

'He would have done it if I hadn't.' Kennedy grinned. 'Someone had to stop Mike's mouth before he went too far, so bear that in mind, Frank, and take a grip. I heard that you've been running off at the mouth about certain things that are best forgotten.'

'Now you're threatening me!' Bartram reached for the pistol nestling in a holster strapped to the right side of his wheel chair and jerked it clear of leather. He cocked the gun and covered Kennedy.

'Don't be a damned fool, Frank,' Kennedy said harshly. 'Put that away. Are you loco? You're scared of the past, but instead of staying away from it you're acting like a fool. If someone sees you pointing a gun at me there'll be questions asked.'

'Go on, get out of here,' Bartram rapped. 'And stay away from me in future, Buck.'

Kennedy gazed at Bartram for an interminable moment, able to see the hotelier's hand trembling. The black muzzle of his pistol wavered. Kennedy shook his head and turned away, untied the stallion and swung into the saddle. He let the animal run, and dust flew as they left town. His thoughts were running deep. He needed to take care of the Paston brothers before Floyd showed up. He did not think Floyd had gained any good sense during his time in prison, and he meant to save his only son from making the same mistake twice. Floyd did not know it yet but he was going to take over the Lazy P ranch and settle down to a quiet life. But before that event arrived something would have to be done about Frank Bartram. The fool was on the same trail Mike Paston had taken, and Paston had died because he suffered conscience trouble after the Mulejaw job. Now it was only too plain that Bartram had to be stopped.

He reined in on the outskirts of town and rode in behind a derelict barn beside the trail. Drawing his Winchester from its saddle boot, he left the stallion tied to a post. When he looked back along the street from a corner of the barn he saw Bartram still seated in his wheel-chair in the doorway of the hotel. He jacked a cartridge into the breech of his rifle and sighted the 44.40 on Bartram's huddled figure. When his foresight centred on Bartram's chest he fired. Bartram jumped under the impact of the bullet and fell back in the wheelchair. Kennedy fired a second shot before running back to the stallion, and he was in the saddle and riding hard for a nearby gully before the echoes of the shooting faded.

Cole wiped sweat from his forehead and reloaded his pistol with cartridges from the loops in his belt. Mart was shooting steadily, making sure of his aim before squeezing his trigger. Cole had recognized Buster Askew as one of the men attacking them, and waited for a chance to put a slug into the BK gun hand. The sun was blazing down mercilessly, its glare highlighting the range. Gun smoke drifted on the hot breeze and echoes rolled through illimitable space.

When the shooting dwindled to sporadic shots, Cole tried to size up the situation.

'What do you reckon triggered Kennedy into action, Mart?'

'It's obvious he wants to settle some old business before Floyd returns.' Mart ducked as a slug whined past his head. 'But Floyd is a marked man now. The law will be watching his every move.'

'Pete Horden ain't much of a lawman,' mused Cole. 'I've had a good chance of getting to know him real well since I became a deputy. I reckon folks in town would be shocked if they knew Horden ran with an outlaw gang before he became a sheriff.'

'Did he tell you that?'

'Not in so many words, but he talked a lot, especially when he'd had a few drinks. I soon put two and two together, and I reckon he's still on the take.'

'Him and Buck Kennedy have always been thick as thieves,' observed Mart. 'Horden put a lot of pressure on me when Floyd was jailed for trying to shoot me. He wanted me to change my statement to clear Floyd. He even offered me money to do it. I reckon I've done well to stay healthy these past three years.'

Cole watched Buster Askew change position and raised his Colt in readiness for a shot. He saw another of the BK outfit move out to the left.

'Watch them, Mart,' he warned. 'It looks like they are gonna try and outflank us.'

'Why don't you move round to your right?' Mart replied. 'I can hold them down from here. If you get Askew, the others will high-tail it. It looks like they ain't trying to kill us. They are holding us down for some reason. I'm wondering where Buck Kennedy went. It ain't like him to start trouble and not finish it. He's up to something that will prove to be bad for us.'

Cole checked his gun. 'Watch your left,' he warned, and slithered away to his right.

Mart resumed firing and the shooting increased. Cole slipped into a shallow depression that angled toward the position occupied by the BK outfit. He covered a dozen yards before removing his Stetson and risking a look above his cover. He saw gun smoke drifting from two positions and realized that Buster Askew had withdrawn from the attack. He remained motionless, studying the ground to the right of Askew's last position, and presently caught a glimpse of the gunman's hat showing intermittently as Askew slithered around Mart's position.

Cole eased out to his own right and within minutes he had outflanked the gun man. He stayed down in cover while Askew crawled steadily into his arc of fire. Askew was moving fast. He approached Cole from the right, pausing frequently to check his position. In the background three guns were shooting steadily – Mart's rifle and the pistols of the other two BK gunnies. Askew eased into a position in front of where Cole was crouching. The gun man was gripping his Colt in his right hand. He paused about six feet from Cole and craned upward to take a look around.

'That's far enough, Buster,' Cole called harshly. 'Throw your gun away and stay still. I've got you covered.'

Askew froze. His gun was pointing away from Cole, and he knew from the direction of Cole's voice that he was at a big disadvantage. But he began to ease his muzzle round in preparation for his next move.

'You'd better do like you're told,' Cole said. 'Get rid of your gun or I'll kill you.'

Askew remained motionless for a couple of moments, and then tossed his gun away. He turned his head toward Cole and grinned.

'It looks like you're smarter than I figured,' he said.

'You need to get a lot smarter than you are.' Cole replied. 'Call your two saddle pards and tell them to get the hell out of here. Get to your feet and tell them. Don't try anything. You are standing on the brink right now.'

Askew heaved a sighed. He stared into the gaping muzzle of Cole's pistol for a moment, then pushed himself to his feet.

'Hey, Carney, Quirk,' he called. 'Quit shooting and ride

out of here.'

The shooting ceased and an uneasy silence settled over the range. Cole did not show himself until he heard the beat of receding hoofs. When he stood up he saw the two gun men were riding off in the direction of BK. Askew stood with his hands at his sides, watching Cole.

'What happens now?' he asked.

'I have a feeling it'll be a waste of time taking you to jail,' Cole replied. 'I figure Buck Kennedy set you to hold us out here while he headed into town. He's an old friend of the sheriff, and Kennedy wouldn't start trouble unless he was covered from the law. So I reckon we'll head for Bar G. One of you gunnies shot Lance Gifford, and I reckon it will be a good idea to let Hank Gifford deal with you.'

'You're a deputy sheriff,' Askew said harshly. 'You ain't supposed to hand a prisoner over to anyone.'

'Gifford will take right good care of you if I ask him nicely.' Cole grinned. 'Let's get your horse, huh?'

Hoofs sounded to Cole's left and he glanced up to see Mart riding over.

'You should have killed the skunk,' said Mart, covering Askew with his rifle.

'You can watch him, and shoot him if he gives you any trouble,' Cole replied. 'Get him mounted while I check Lance. We'll head for Bar G.'

'Anything will be better than going on to town,' replied Mart. 'If Kennedy has ridden in to see the sheriff then we'll be in real trouble if we show up there.'

Cole went back to where Lance Gifford was stretched out in the grass.

'How you doing, Lance?' he asked. 'Do you feel up to

35

riding back to Bar G? I think you'd be safer there than in town. We've got Buster Askew, and I want to leave him with your pa while I check out the situation.'

'Sure.' Lance nodded. His face was pale and he was clearly shocked, but his jaw was set and his eyes held the glint of determination. 'Take me home, Cole.'

Cole helped the youngster into his saddle. Lance stifled a groan and slumped but took up his reins and turned his horse. Mart came back to them, accompanied by Askew, who was leading Bill Mason's horse. Mart was holding a pistol in his right hand. Cole remained by Lance's side, and watched the youngster anxiously as they rode north-east towards the distant Bar G. He was taking no chances, and watched their surroundings alertly as they continued across the undulating range.

They passed Lazy P. Mart looked long and hard at the ranch buildings, then suddenly reined in and turned to Cole.

'I can't help thinking we're making a mistake leaving the spread deserted,' he said. 'I reckon I oughta stay here, just in case more trouble comes up.' He turned his attention to the sullen Askew. 'What about it, Buster?' he demanded. 'What's Kennedy up to? Why is your outfit on the war path?'

'Do you expect me to know what's in Buck's mind?' Askew shook his head. 'All I know is that you started the shooting at your place this morning. You killed Bill Mason in cold blood.'

'So that's the way you're playing it,' Cole cut in angrily. 'I saw you with Mason across the stream when the shooting started. You couldn't have seen what happened because I shot Mason after he fired at us. You took off

36

when Mason went down, and you must have met up with
Kennedy out of our sight. So what orders did he give you?
I don't believe you just turned up out of the blue and
started shooting at us. You're in a lot of trouble right now,
so you'd better come clean.'

'You'll have to talk to Kennedy to find out what's going
on. I've got nothing to say.' Askew shrugged his thick
shoulders, and then shook his head. 'I know what I saw.
Mart fired first and Mason went down.'

'Perhaps you don't realize the bad trouble you're in,'
said Mart, levelling his pistol at Askew. 'You've been
tossing lead at us. You shot Lance, and he's like to die if he
don't get some treatment. If he kicks off it will mean a
rope around your neck, Askew. So you'd better tell us what
we need to know.'

'Heck, you know we weren't trying to kill you,' growled
Askew. 'You and your brother would be dead now if that
was the case. We were just keeping you pinned down.'

'And while you were doing that, Kennedy rode into
town to talk to Pete Horden, huh?' Cole surmised. 'So
what gives with Kennedy and Horden? They go back a
long way, and they are thick as molasses. From time to time
I've heard Horden hint at his past, and although he never
painted himself black, I learned enough to know that he
should never have been elected as a law man.'

'You can think what you like.' Askew grimaced and
shrugged his thick shoulders. 'It won't amount to anything. I did what I had to and you know you are in big
trouble. Someone has got to pay for Floyd going to jail;
and guess who's been elected?'

Mart swung his pistol and slammed the long barrel
against the side of Askew's head. The gunman uttered a

cry and pitched sideways out of his saddle. His horse was startled and tried to bolt but Cole reached out a long arm and grabbed its reins. Mart vacated his saddle quickly and bent over Askew as the gunman tried to get to his feet. He dropped to one knee beside Askew, jammed the muzzle of his Colt against Askew's throat, and grabbed Askew's shirt-front with his free hand.

'You're the one in bad trouble,' Mart rasped. 'You're lying through your teeth about how Mason died, and you've been tossing slugs at us. I'd rather take you along face down across your saddle, so wise up to yourself and start playing ball. If we are going down on your say-so then we won't go alone. We'll take as many of you as we can.'

'Lay off, Mart,' Cole rapped. 'We've got more than enough trouble without you making it worse. Take a look at that ridge to the north. I spotted movement there and I reckon some more of Kennedy's hardcases are about to show up. I want you to ride on to Bar G and tell Hank Gifford what is going on.'

'And what are you gonna do?' demanded Mart.

'What I'm paid to do,' Cole replied grimly. 'I'll cover you from here and hold up any of Kennedy's crew, if they try anything.'

Mart motioned for Askew to mount up and then set off. Cole turned to face the ridge, and when two riders appeared he rode towards them, his law badge glinting on his chest.

THREE

Carney and Quirk rode behind the nearest ridge when Askew told them to quit the fight. Quirk swung out of his saddle and crawled forward to watch Cole and Mart Paston. Carney sat his horse in cover, shaking his head.

'We can pick them off from here,' said Quirk, and got up to take his rifle out of its scabbard.

'The hell we can!' Carney shook his head. 'You heard what Kennedy said. Don't kill them until we get the word from him. So pull in your horns and we'll ride back to the spread. Those two Pastons are hot stuff with their shooting irons. We're on a beating to nothing, just trying to hold them up.'

'Buster will be madder than a wet hen if we don't get him away from them,' Quirk mused.

'Well, I ain't going against Kennedy's orders.' Carney spoke fiercely. 'We'd have to kill the Pastons to stop them, and that ain't on the cards yet. Let's move out. Our best bet is to ride to town and talk to Kennedy. What do you say?'

'OK.' Quirk got to his feet and slid his long gun back into its scabbard. He led his horse back from the crest. "It looks like the Pastons are heading for the Gifford spread. Lance Gifford has been hit. If they take Askew to Big G he could be in real trouble. Since Kennedy horse-whipped Lance, Hank Gifford has been breathing fire. He's gonna cut loose one of these days, and then we'll get it in the neck.'

'Stop belly-aching. We get paid to take risks.' Carney grinned. 'What do you want to do – ride into town or back to BK?'

Quirk shook his head. 'It won't do to ride back to head-quarters. Kennedy will expect us to shadow the Pastons and check on their movements. You know what he's like if we disobey orders.'

'So we'll follow them, and ride into town later,' Carney grated. 'If we play our cards right we can be in a saloon this evening.'

'I doubt it. Kennedy will push us now he's started dishing out trouble.'

They remained in cover and watched Cole and Mart Paston cross the range in the direction of Big G. Quirk was keen to obey Kennedy's orders, and so long as the Pastons continued to ride in the opposite direction to town he was content to follow. But Carney wanted to visit Squaw Creek, and long before they reached Big G he began to belly-ache for a change of plan.

'You can see where they are headed,' he said. 'There is only Big G out this way. We're wasting time now. We should turn around and high-tail it to town. Kennedy must have left there by now, and is probably looking for us.'

'What about Askew; do we just leave him?'

'Cole Paston is a deputy sheriff, and Buster is his pris-oner. Law men don't let go of their prisoners for any reason. So Buster will wind up in the town jail, and we can always bust him out of there later.'

'So we'll head for town.' Quirk swung his horse. 'Come on, let's go find the boss.'

They headed in the direction of the distant town, and had barely rejoined the trail to Squaw Creek when Carney spotted a rider approaching.

'There's Kennedy now,' he said. 'You can't mistake that big white stallion he rides. If he's gonna make more trouble on this range then he oughta change to a horse that can't be recognized.'

Buck Kennedy pulled the stallion down to a canter when he recognized his two men.

'Where's Askew?' he flung at them as they reined in, and cursed when they had explained. 'Now you know why I try to handle everything myself,' he said. 'How in hell did Askew get caught?'

'Just bad luck, boss,' said Quirk. 'You want us to spring him loose from that deputy?'

'Only if you can catch them before they hit Big G, otherwise it will be too late. Once they spread the word about what happened today we'll have a big fight on our hands. So go get 'em and shoot the hell out of them. With them dead and buried we'll hold a winning hand. Tell Askew I want them out of it before he reports back to me at the spread. Have you got that?'

'Sure, boss.' Carney nodded. 'You don't have to spell it out. We were doing a good job holding the Pastons until Askew got too clever and was caught. Cole Paston was too sharp for him.'

'See that Cole Paston ain't too clever for you,' responded Kennedy. 'You'll be well paid for this job if you do it right. Now get going. And if the Pastons do reach Big G then don't come back to my ranch because you'll be out of a job.'

Carney swung his horse and used his spurs. Quirk followed him closely. Kennedy watched them until they dropped from sight beyond a ridge before giving the stallion its head and continuing to BK.

'We'll never make it,' Quirk protested as he and Carney burned up the range back the way they had come.

'The Pastons weren't travelling fast,' said Carney. 'We'll get them. Push that fleabag of yours and see if it can hit a gallop. They are still a couple of hours from Big G, and so long as we catch them out of earshot of Big G we'll be able to get the job done.'

An hour later they reined on a crest and saw Cole and Mart Paston just ahead. Askew was tied in his saddle, with the lead rope of the horse carrying Bill Mason's body hitched to his saddle horn. Lance Gifford was slumped over the neck of his horse. Cole Paston was riding behind the others, and they could tell by his attitude that he was alert to his surroundings. Carney pulled his horse back from the crest and called to Quirk to follow him.

Carney rode fast in cover to pull ahead of the Pastons. Quirk was hard put to stay with him, but at length Carney reined up to a crest, and when he looked for the Pastons he saw that he and Quirk had gained considerably on their quarry. His eyes glittered as he weighed the situation.

'We won't get a better chance than this,' Carney declared. 'They are still a long way from Big G. We'll wait until they pull level with us and then go for them.'

'Cole Paston has seen us,' said Quirk. 'Heck, he's coming this way.'

42

Carney clenched his teeth when he saw Cole turning towards the spot where they were sitting their mounts.

'OK,' he snarled. 'Let's stop wasting time and get the job done. Kick that nag of yours into life and let's go. Take the deputy first, and then go straight for Mart Paston. He won't know what's hit him.'

Cole Paston was cantering towards them, sunlight glinting on the pistol in his right hand. Carney touched spurs to his mount and sent the animal off the crest and down the slope. He drew his Colt and cocked it. Quirk followed closely on his heels. Carney saw that Mart Paston was continuing in the direction of Big G, and he was satisfied with the situation. The two Pastons had split up.

Cole recognized Carney as the distance closed between them. When Carney lifted his pistol to start shooting, Cole snapped off a quick shot. The pistol kicked against the heel of his hand and gunsmoke flared. Echoes hammered away into the distance. Carney felt a stunning blow in his right shoulder and was dimly aware of his gun spinning out of his hand. He snatched at the butt of his rifle but his right hand did not operate normally. His fingers refused to close around the stock of the long gun. Cole fired again. Carney was hit in the forehead and his world exploded and vanished. He fell sideways and pitched out of his saddle.

Quirk was shocked when Carney went down, and swung his horse to flee. Cole was thirty yards away and closing fast. Quirk realized he had no chance to get away and reined in quickly. He twisted in his saddle and lifted his gun into the aim. Gun echoes were drifting away across the range and the hammering thud of Cole's horse as it approached beat out a deadly rhythm. Quirk squeezed his trigger and saw Cole duck. Smoke flared from Cole's gun. His shot narrowly missed, and Quirk heard the slug crackle past his right ear. He triggered his gun in a frenzied attempt to put Cole down.

Cole fired again. Quirk's horse staggered with a slug in its chest. The animal went down quickly, throwing Quirk's gun off aim. Quirk kicked his feet clear of his stirrups and hit the ground beside the horse. He lost his grip on his pistol and then his face hit the ground. He rolled quickly and got to his feet, peering around for his gun. Seeing the weapon in the grass, he lunged forward to pounce on it, and as his fingers closed around the butt he felt a lightning stab of pain in his belly. He lost all interest in his gun and fell on his face in the lush grass.

Cole could feel pain in his left forearm where one of Quirk's slugs had caught him, but he was not disabled, and reined in when he reached Quirk, who was lying motionless on his face. He sprang from his saddle and kicked Quirk's gun away. When he pulled Quirk over on to his back he saw that the gunman was dead. He straightened and cuffed sweat from his forehead. He glanced at Carney, saw blood on the man's forehead, and did not need to check him out. Carney was dead.

Aware that blood was streaming from a deep bullet gash in his forearm, Cole holstered his pistol and removed his neckerchief to use it as a bandage, tying it tightly around the wound. He climbed back in his saddle and rode after Mart without a backward glance at the two men he had killed. Mart had reined in and was waiting for him.

'Quirk and Carney,' Mart said. 'I recognized them.'

'They're both dead,' Cole replied. 'They couldn't leave well alone. Let's get on.'

When Lance Gifford's horse started moving forward again the youngster fell out of his saddle; he was unconscious when Cole bent over him.

'He's done well,' Mart observed, 'but he ain't going any further under his own steam, that's for sure. Shall I ride on to Big G and get a wagon out for him? He ain't gonna sit his saddle any more today.'

'That sounds like a good idea.' Cole nodded. 'As soon as Hank Gifford gets here I'll head into town and get a posse out for Buck Kennedy.'

Mart spurred his horse and rode off in the direction of Big G. Cole dismounted and bent over Lance Gifford, who was still unconscious. He made the youngster as comfortable as possible, but there was little he could do about the wound Lance had suffered. He straightened and turned to Buster Askew. The gunman was watching him closely.

'What's on your mind, Askew?' Cole demanded.

'I was thinking that you don't have a chance against this set-up,' Askew replied. 'I'll do a deal with you. I'll tell you what is going on if you'll turn me loose. I reckon it's the only way you can save your life. There are big odds building up, and you and your brother will finish up with your faces in the dust if you don't get wise to the situation.'

'I reckon you're bluffing,' said Cole. 'You know that if Lance dies you'll be charged with his murder.'

'I didn't shoot him,' retorted Askew. 'It was Quirk that nailed him.'

'And Quirk is dead so he can't deny it.' Cole smiled tensely. 'But you wouldn't be able to prove you didn't fire the shot, and I reckon a jury would hang you, especially with my evidence.'

'That wouldn't help you and your brother. You better

45

think about what I've said. Leave it too late and you'll be sorry.'

Cole sat down on a knoll and tried to relax. He was impatient to get back to town and set the wheels in motion for the arrest of Buck Kennedy. He considered what Askew had told him and believed the gunman was lying in order to escape arrest. This trouble had started more than three years ago, and no one seemed to know its origins. Mart had shot Frank Bartram, the hotelier in town, but Bartram had not made any charge, and Mart had not said a word about the incident. Then Floyd had tried to shoot Mart, and went to prison for three years. Floyd had always been a troublemaker. But now he was on his way back to the range, and trouble was flaring again.

An hour passed before Cole heard the beat of approaching hoofs. He got to his feet and dropped a hand to his pistol, but recognized the two riders he saw coming toward him. Mart was returning with Hank Gifford, Lance's father. The riders pulled up in a cloud of dust and Hank sprang from his saddle. He was a short, fleshy man with wide shoulders and thick, powerful arms. His expression showed that he feared the worst as he dropped to his knees beside his prostrate son.

'I don't think his life is in danger,' observed Cole. 'Now you're here, Hank, I'll head for town and send the doc out to your place.'

Hank Gifford got to his feet and turned to Askew, who was still tied to his horse.

'Did you shoot my boy?' he demanded, dropping his hand to the butt of his gun.

'Take it easy,' warned Cole. 'Askew is my prisoner.'

'I've had my fill of Kennedy and his outfit,' Hank

grated. 'It's about time BK was taught a lesson. Buck Kennedy has ridden roughshod around this range as long as I can remember, but now he's reached the end of his rope, and I'm gonna see he gets what he's been asking for.'

'Leave it for now,' Cole replied. 'I wanta take out a posse for Buck Kennedy. You better concentrate on Lance. Have you got a wagon coming out for him?'

Hank Gifford nodded. He did not take his eyes off Buster Askew, and eagerness was showing plainly in his expression.

'Mart, stick around here with Hank and go to Big G with him when the wagon arrives,' Cole directed his brother. 'I'll head for town with Askew, and I'll come back to you with a posse and the doctor.'

'I think I oughta head back to Lazy P,' protested Mart.

'It won't be safe for you to ride alone after what's happened,' Cole growled impatiently. 'Just do like I tell you, huh? I don't need to worry about you. I'll be out at Big G as fast as I can make it, and then we'll tackle Buck Kennedy. In any case, Hank shouldn't be left here alone with Lance. You need to be on hand in case any more of the BK outfit show up looking for trouble.'

'OK.' Mart was not pleased, but drew his rifle and sat down on the knoll Cole had vacated.

Cole swung into his saddle and took hold of Askew's reins. He turned in the direction of the distant town, leading Askew's horse. Mason's horse was tethered to Askew's saddle horn by its reins, and followed closely as they departed. Cole glanced at the setting sun and realized it would be late by the time he reached Squaw Creek. He pushed on as fast as he could, and watched his surroundings alertly as he rode.

Askew tried to engage him in conversation but Cole was not in the mood and Askew fell silent. They continued steadily. The sun went down in a grand display of red and gold fire, and the heat of the long day faded slowly. The sky darkened and stars began to show. Cole knew the range intimately and pushed on with grim determination. When he finally sighted the lights of Squaw Creek he straightened his shoulders, brought his mind back to full alertness, and fought off tiredness and hunger.

'Have you thought about doing a deal?' demanded Askew.

'No deal,' replied Cole as they rode along the broad street to the law office.

Askew made no reply and Cole reined in at the hitch rail in front of the jail. He stepped down from his saddle and tethered the horse. There was a light in the big office window but the street door was locked. He reached into a pocket for his key, unlocked the door, and then went for Askew, who could not dismount until he had been untied. Cole drew his pistol and held it ready in his right hand while he loosened the rope binding his prisoner. Askew grinned as he dismounted, and seemed to lose his balance as his feet hit the dust of the street. Cole reached out with his left hand to steady him, and the gunman swung round, his left arm lifting to block Cole's gun hand.

Cole, although anticipating trouble, was caught flat-footed by Askew's move. He felt Askew's left hand grasp his gun hand, and the weapon was almost jerked from his grasp. Askew threw a right hand punch at Cole's jaw. Cole lifted his shoulder and blocked the blow. Askew was a big man, taller even than Cole, and he carried a lot of weight.

He fancied himself as a fist fighter, and Cole had seen him in action around town of a Saturday night. But Cole fancied his chances against most men, and lowered his head to protect his chin. He punched with his left fist while using his strength to retain his grip on his pistol.

Askew expected Cole to hang on to his pistol and used both hands to try and twist the gun out of Cole's grasp. Cole threw a tight left hook and felt his knuckles crash against Askew's chin. Askew's knees buckled, and he fought desperately to stay on his feet. Cole used his weight to crowd Askew back against the nearest horse and, as the gunman was brought to a halt against the animal, Cole jerked his head forward in a vicious butt. His forehead made contact with Askew's nose and blood spurted. Askew yelled in pain and changed his tactics. His left knee lifted to Cole's belly.

Cole stamped on Askew's right foot, threw his left arm around Askew's neck, and used his strength to wrestle the gunman to the ground. Askew lost his grip on Cole's gun and fell heavily. His head struck the edge of the sidewalk, he uttered a groan and relaxed instantly. Cole moved in, his gun ready. Askew was unconscious. Cole holstered his gun and grasped Askew's collar, ignoring the pain in his left forearm. He dragged the gunman into the law office. Askew was a mess. Blood covered most of his face. His mouth gaped and he was breathing heavily. When his eyes flickered open he gazed vacantly at Cole.

'If you've had enough then we'll get down to business,' said Cole. 'On your feet, Buster, and sit on the chair by the desk. Empty your pockets on the desk and I'll book you.'

Askew made two attempts to get off the floor and Cole, losing patience, dragged him up and thrust him into a chair. At that moment the street door was opened and Sheriff Horden came into the office. Cole looked up, and was shocked to see blood and bruises on Horden's face.

'What happened to you, Pete?' demanded Cole.

'A couple of hardcases roughed me up earlier. I heard they were in the saloon, and when I went to check them out they turned nasty and set about me. One of them held a gun while the other hit me. I was knocked cold. Both were strangers. When I came to they had gone. I've just checked through the town for them but it looks like they've pulled out.'

'So I'm not the only one to get trouble today,' mused Cole.

'I've heard about your trouble.' Horden wiped blood from his face. 'Buck Kennedy was in this afternoon. He said Mart shot Bill Mason in cold blood.'

'He lied to you,' Cole responded. 'I shot Mason after he fired at Mart and me. It'll be easy to check out whose story is right. Mart was using a .44.40 Winchester and I shot Mason with my .45.'

'And you've arrested Askew.' Horden was grim-faced; his eyes held a hard glint.

Cole explained the grim events of the day, then said tiredly, 'I want to take out a posse and pick up Buck Kennedy. He's running wild out there on the range. And Doc Carmody is needed out at Big G. Lance Gifford might die if he doesn't get medical treatment.'

'Did you see who shot young Gifford?'

'Not the first time, but Askew was with other BK riders, and when they started shooting at us Lance was hit again. That's why Askew is under arrest.'

'And you killed Quirk and Carney. We had trouble in

50

town earlier. Frank Bartram was sitting in the doorway of the hotel in his wheelchair when someone shot him dead.'

'The hell you say! Did you get the killer?'

'No! The shots were not heard. My guess is that they were fired from the edge of town. Bartram was found slumped in his chair with two slugs in his chest. Where was Mart around three this afternoon? He's known for carrying a rifle. I've never seen him wear a pistol, and he's gone around these last three years with a chip on his shoulder.'

'You can forget about Mart.' Cole said sharply. 'He hasn't been alone since noon. When I left him to come back to town he was with Hank Gifford, and should be at Big G until I return there. You'll have to look elsewhere for Bartram's killer.'

'I'm not forgetting that Mart shot Bartram three years ago.' Horden grimaced and a trickle of blood dribbled from his left nostril. He dabbed at it with a stained handkerchief.

'That was a stand-up fight, and Mart never carried a pistol afterwards,' observed Cole.

'I'm not happy with the way the situation is panning out.' Horden grimaced. 'Floyd Kennedy went to jail for three years for trying to kill Mart. So what was that all about?'

'You know as much about it as I do,' returned Cole.

'The point is, Cole, I'm thinking of suspending you from duty.' Horden did not meet Cole's gaze but fiddled with papers on the desk.

'Heck, I want to get on with fighting the trouble now it has started,' said Cole. 'It's obvious what is going on. If I bring in Buck Kennedy the trouble will stop.'

Horden shook his head and sighed. 'I can't let you do

51

that, Cole. You're an interested party in this trouble, and whatever happened today at your spread, all I have to go on is your word against Buck Kennedy's, and you know that kind of evidence won't stand up in court. I'm gonna have to handle this myself, and I want you well out of it until I've finished.'

'So I'm suspended, huh?' Cole looked into the sheriff's battered face and saw much that he did not like. Horden looked sick, and not because of his facial injuries. 'I get it,' he mused. 'Buck Kennedy has got at you, huh?' He nodded slowly. 'I can see what's going on. I don't need to ask whose side you are on, Sheriff. OK.' He removed the law star from his shirtfront and tossed it on the desk, where it lay glinting in the lamplight. 'I'll leave it to you then, and I hope you know what you're doing.'

Cole turned to the door, where he paused and glanced back over his shoulder. He saw Askew sitting up straight in his seat, grinning. Cole shook his head and stepped out through the doorway. As he pulled the door to, the shadows on the street were tattered by orange gun flashes, and the silence of the night was shattered by raucous gunfire.

FOUR

Cole flung himself forward out of the office doorway as slugs thudded into the woodwork around him. He went down heavily on the sidewalk, dimly aware that three guns were shooting from the dense shadows across the street. A lightning flash of pain caught him at the outer edge of his left shoulder and he clenched his teeth as he jerked his pistol from its holster and returned fire. Gunsmoke blew back into his face. He heard glass shattering above him, and realized that not all of the shooting was directed at him. Shards of the big front window of the law office came crashing down on the sidewalk.

He concentrated on the gun flashes across the street. Muzzle flame was streaking the shadows. His big pistol bucked in his hand. His first two shots bracketed the alley opposite, and the gun there cut out instantly. Then a slug tore a splinter out of the sidewalk beside his right shoulder. He rolled to the left, came back into the aim, and fired two shots at the gun flashes stabbing at him from the doorway of the dress shop opposite the law office. He rolled again and fell off the sidewalk into the dust of the street. When he came back into the aim the shooting had ceased and echoes were grumbling away across the town. He exhaled deeply to rid his protesting lungs of gunsmoke and reloaded his gun.

His ears were ringing from the noise of the shooting. He remained motionless, covering the shadows opposite, his ears strained. He heard the sound of running footsteps receding in one of the alleys opposite, but did not move immediately. It could be a trap. He looked up at the front of the office and saw that the big window had disintegrated. He got to one knee, his gun ready, but the movement did not precipitate another attack and he got cautiously to his feet.

He took a final look across the street, satisfied himself that the attackers had departed, and went back to the office. The door was ajar and he pushed it wide, wondering why the sheriff had not taken a hand in the shooting. Then he saw Horden stretched out on the floor beside the desk with Buster Askew bent over him and in the act of taking the gun from the sheriff's holster.

'You don't need the gun, Askew,' rapped Cole. The gunman froze, then looked up sideways, grinning a smile that looked forced and unreal. Cole grinned harshly. 'Get up and put your hands up.'

Askew hesitated for a moment, and then straightened and raised his hands shoulder high. Cole cocked his gun and entered the office.

'Who was doing the shooting?' demanded Askew.

'I suspect it was some of your pards. I didn't get a look at anyone but I'll run them down. Pick up those keys on the desk and lock yourself in a cell; I wanta check the sheriff. It looks like he's been bad hit.'

'I'll go for the doc,' Askew said.

'You'll do like you're told. Get moving.'

Askew shrugged and lowered his hands. He picked up the big bunch of keys lying on the desk top and led the way into the cell block out back. He unlocked the door of a cell, left the key in the lock, and entered the cage. Cole slammed the door and locked it. He locked the connecting door on his way back to the office and put the bunch of keys in his pocket. The sheriff had not moved on the floor. He was lying on his face and there was blood on the back of his shirt just below the right shoulder blade.

Cole turned the sheriff over on to his back, and shook his head when he saw the big bloodstain on the front of Horden's shirt. It didn't look good. He started for the street door, but turned and went back to the desk. His law star was still lying where he had tossed it. He picked it up and pinned it back on his shirt. He paused and looked out around the street before stepping on to the sidewalk. Then he halted and moved back inside the office, for Doc Carmody was approaching, with a medical bag in his hand.

Carmody was a short, fleshy man with wide shoulders and a big paunch. He was wearing a dark-blue town suit and a flat-crowned grey Stetson. In his late fifties, he walked with a slight limp, favouring his left leg, which had been broken many years before. He came into the office wrinkling his nose at the stench of burned powder.

'I was just coming for you, Doc,' said Cole, as he stepped aside and pointed to the motionless sheriff. 'Pete looks bad to me.'

Carmody went to Horden's side and bent to make a swift examination. He straightened, shaking his head. 'It looks like I've got a tough chore on my hands but I might be able to save him. He's a hard man.' He went back to the door and peered out. 'Hey, Jake, get a couple of men and bring them here. I need some help to take a patient over to my place.'

'OK, Doc,' a voice replied from the street. 'Who has been shot?'

'You can take a look at him when you've carried him to my office,' Carmody replied, turning back to Cole. 'What happened, Cole? Who did the shooting?'

'That's what I mean to find out. I'll leave you here, Doc, and check with you later about the sheriff. But I need to tell you before I forget. Lance Gifford is out at Big G. He's got a couple of slugs in him so he'll need your help. It looks like being a busy time for you, huh?'

'I'll have to work on the sheriff before I think of leaving town. I'll be as quick as I can with Pete. You want I should lock the door when I leave?' Carmody asked.

Cole shook his head. 'Don't bother,' he replied. 'I'll get Charlie Swain to put in a new front window.'

'You've got blood on your shirt in two places,' Carmody observed.

Cole shrugged his right shoulder and then turned away. 'It ain't serious. You can look at me later.'

He went out to the sidewalk, drawing his gun as he did so, and crossed the street. The ambushers were long gone, he knew, but he had to start somewhere in his search for them. Three guns had shot up the office, and he wondered about the two strangers who had beaten the sheriff earlier. He moved through the shadows on the opposite side of the street, checking out the two alleys from where the shots had been fired. He did not expect to find anything, and was not disappointed. He stood in the darkened doorway of the dress shop and looked around the street. His assailants had departed from the scene of the shooting by way of the alleys leading to the back lots, and he did not intend wasting time searching every square inch of the town. He went along the street, keeping to the denser shadows, and paused outside the livery barn on the edge of town.

A lantern was suspended from a hook over the centre of the big open doorway and a small circle of yellow light was cast upon the dusty ground directly beneath it. Cole skirted the shaft of light and slipped inside the big barn. There was another lantern burning in the small office to the left of the doorway, and he went forward cautiously to find Pete Welton, the liveryman, seated at his dusty desk.

'Hi, Pete,' called Cole.

Welton started nervously, swinging around in his seat. He reached for a double-barrelled shotgun which was lying on the desk within reach.

'Oh, it's you, Cole,' he said. 'You startled me. I didn't hear you come in.'

'What's made you nervous?' demanded Cole.

'A couple of hardcases – strangers – showed up earlier. They put their nags in a stall and refused to pay me for their keep – said they'd settle with me before they rode out. You know I don't do business that way, and when I told them one pulled his hogleg and stuck it under my nose. For a moment there I thought he meant to blow my head off, but he simmered down some when the other guy said they had another job to do. They left their horses and went off along the street.'

'Didn't you report them to Horden?'

'They told me to stay here, and I wasn't about to cross

them up. The one who threatened to shoot me looked like he'd kill his grandmother if she spoke out of turn.'

'And two strangers roughed up the sheriff earlier,' mused Cole. 'They could be two of the three men I'm looking for. When did those hardcases show up here?'

'They came in about four hours ago.' Welton consulted his pocket watch. 'I went past Brady's saloon about two hours after that and saw them in there, drinking like they just walked across the Mojave Desert. What do you want them for?'

'Can you describe them?'

'They were a couple of real hardcases, like I said. One was tall; the other a lot shorter. Both were dressed in range clothes. The tall one was wearing a light-blue shirt – the other had on a green one. The shorter one was wearing twin pistols on a couple of crossed cartridge belts. Looking at them, I got the impression they were gunnies out on a job.'

'Are their horses still in the barn?'

'No. The short guy came in about an hour ago and took both mounts. When I asked for money he put his hands on his guns and asked me if I'd take gold, silver or lead. I didn't argue with him and he went off with the nags.'

'I reckon I know what job they had in mind,' mused Cole. 'They jumped the sheriff. And I was ambushed by three guns a few minutes ago. The sheriff was hit in the shooting.'

'Is he dead?' Welton's expression changed and shock appeared on his weathered face.

'Doc reckons he'll live. I'll see Brady. Perhaps he can throw light on the strangers.'

Cole departed and paused in the shadows around the

livery barn. He looked along the length of the main street, which was deceptively quiet, but sensed an atmosphere of hostility in the deep shadows. Had the three gunnies been after him or the sheriff? He considered the question and came to the conclusion that the shooting had been intended to kill the local law, including him. The three strangers would have seen him clearly as he stepped out of the law office, and if the sheriff had been their specific target they would have held their fire until they had him squarely in their sights.

He walked along the boardwalk to Brady's saloon, and paused to one side of the batwings to glance inside before showing himself. There were no strangers present. He saw Joe Brady behind the long bar, chatting to Al Bennett, the bartender. He pushed through the swing doors and crossed to the bar. Brady looked up, saw him, and came along the bar to confront him.

'I heard the shooting,' said Brady, taking a cigar out of his thick-lipped mouth. He was middle-aged, short and of heavy build – running to seed. His large face was fleshy, especially around his eyes, and he was making a good start towards a double chin. His blue-grey eyes peered at Cole through a network of fine wrinkles, and were almost concealed by heavy greying eyebrows that were growing seemingly out of control. 'How's the sheriff? He was shot, I heard.'

'You heard right.' Cole looked around. 'He should live, Doc reckons. Horden was roughed up in here earlier, Joe. Did you see what happened?'

'Yeah. He was only doing his job – talking to two strangers about where they had come from and what their plans were, and one of them didn't take kindly to his questions. There were no regulars in here at the time, and I picked up my Greener and covered the strangers. Horden was down in the sawdust by then.'

'Did you see a third man around?' Cole asked.

Brady shook his head. 'No, just the two who roughed up the sheriff. They were two hardcases on the prod.'

'Thanks.' Cole turned away. 'I'll keep looking for them.'

'Say, what about Frank Bartram being shot right in front of the hotel?' Brady said. 'Who in hell would gun down a man in a wheelchair?'

'Yeah, it makes you wonder, but more to the point: *why* was he killed?' Cole did not pause and departed from the saloon.

Cole moved into the shadows beside the batwings and looked around the street. Nothing stirred, and a heavy silence pressed against his ears. He considered the incidents that had occurred and wondered what was going on. He guessed it had to do with Floyd Kennedy's return. Buck Kennedy had certainly kicked over the traces today, and Cole needed to pick up the rancher to prevent more trouble. He wondered if Frank Bartram's death had anything to do with Buck Kennedy's visit to the town earlier. And where were the two men who had roughed up the sheriff in Brady's saloon? Had they been involved in the gun attack on the jail, with a third man as yet unknown?

The sound of hoofs entering the street at his back had Cole turning to face the sound. He caught a glimpse of a rider going into the livery barn and eased back into deeper shadow. He slipped into an alley, traversed it to the back lots, and moved silently through the darkness to the livery barn. He reached the corral behind the stable, ducked between two rails to approach the barn by its back door, which was open, and entered silently.

A horse stamped in a stall by the stable office, and then the murmur of low voices sounded. Cole went forward silently until he could see the office door. He frowned when he saw a figure standing in the doorway, chatting to the livery man. He eased closer, saw the figure was that of a female, and shook his head when he recognized the newcomer as Jane Kennedy, daughter of Buck and sister to Floyd.

She was bad trouble at the best of times, thought Cole, and hung back, not wanting to confront her. She was a wildcat where the Pastons were concerned, and Cole was faintly surprised by the realization because there was a time not too long ago when he had thought she was sweet on his brother Mart. But that was before Floyd Kennedy had tried to shoot Mart.

Jane Kennedy left the stable, and paused under the lantern hanging in the big open doorway. Cole watched her impassively as she stood motionless in the circle of yellow lamplight. Jane was a tall, strong girl, fleshy like her father, and she possessed more than her fair share of the Kennedy family temper, which was vile at the best of times. He could see that she was undecided about which way to proceed and that surprised him because she had only one friend in Squaw Creek and that was Polly Ellard, the daughter of Sam Ellard who ran a freight line. Eventually Jane moved off, and Cole followed her at a distance, wanting to check out her destination. With Floyd reputed to be back in the county, Cole wanted to keep a close watch on any and every Kennedy who came into town.

Jane went along the street, her boot heels thudding on

the boardwalk. Cole stayed in the street, making no sound
in the thick dust. When Jane passed by the Ellard house
without so much as a glance at the front door, Cole lengthened his stride and moved in closer behind her. She
reached the end of the sidewalk and stepped down into
the dust. Ahead of her was a shanty town of maybe thirty
cabins, shacks and tents where the labourers of the town
lived in a close community. Cole stayed in the shadows,
wondering now about Jane's destination; and his breathing quickened when the girl went forward unhesitatingly
into dense shadows.

She paused at the door of a shack. Cole remained in
nearby shadows. Jane knocked at the door, and yellow
lamplight streamed out into the night when the door was
opened. Cole saw a face he knew well when the man
greeted the girl and grasped her arm to pull her quickly
into the shack. Jane went willingly and the door closed
abruptly, but not before Cole had recognized the fleshy
features of her brother Floyd.

What the hell was Floyd doing in town unannounced,
and apparently lying low? Cole heard a horse stamp close
by and moved through the shadows to the rear of the
shack that Jane had entered. He paused at the rear corner
and leaned forward to look around the back. A dim light
was shining through a small rear window of the dilapidated building which gave enough light for Cole to see
three horses hitched to a rail. He quickly put two and two
together. Two men had attacked the sheriff, and three
men had set a gun trap at the law office. Cole did not
think he had far to look for the culprits. He edged around
the corner, approached the rear window of the shack, and
peered through the dusty glass.

Jane Kennedy was in the centre of the shack, talking animatedly to Floyd. Two hardcases were sitting at a table watching the proceedings with interest. One was wearing a blue shirt. the other a green one – the two men whom the livery man had described. The sound of voices reached Cole's ears but he could not hear what was being said. He saw Jane pause and look anxiously at Floyd, who shook his head emphatically. Cole wished he could hear their conversation. He eased back from the window, returned to the front corner of the shack, and waited in the shadows for developments. Ten minutes passed before the door of the shack was opened and Jane reappeared. She set off quickly back towards the main street, and did not look back.

Floyd stepped into the doorway of the shack and remained there, staring after his sister. Cole studied Floyd's fleshy face. Three years behind bars did not seem to have changed Floyd at all. His features still carried a sharp look, like that of a fox, or more like a pack-rat, and bad temper was etched in the lines on his forehead.

Cole eased away and went after Jane. He could always come back for the trio in the shack, and he would need gun help before even considering picking them up. He kept to the shadows as he followed Jane, and saw her stop at the Ellard front door. She knocked, and a moment later was admitted. Cole kept going. He went back to the law office, keenly aware that he was alone and without help.

He checked on Buster Askew, who was lying on a bunk in his cell with his hands behind his head. Askew was snoring loudly. Cole shook his head as he went back into the front office. The big front window was smashed and shards of glass were strewn over the floor. He needed a

posse to help with the arrest of Floyd and his two com-
panions, and if he found that Floyd's gun had been fired
recently he would try and tie Floyd into the attempted
murder of Sheriff Horden.

It seemed senseless to lock the front door of the office
with the big window shattered, but he turned the key in
the lock and went along the street to call on some of the
townsmen who usually answered a call for help from the
local law. He paused outside Brady's saloon and peered
over the swing doors. Charlie Swain, one of the town's car-
penters, was standing at the bar chatting with Brady. Cole
entered and approached Swain, a tall, fair-haired man
with a drooping moustache adorning his top lip.

'Howdy, Cole,' said Swain. 'I just heard about the
sheriff. Is he gonna be OK?'

'I don't know yet, Charlie. Doc reckons he'll live. We'll
just have to wait and see. Can you give me a hand for half
an hour?'

'What's doing?' Swain gulped down his glass of beer
and wiped his mouth on his sleeve.

'I think I can lay my hands on the two men that shot the
sheriff,' Cole said. 'They're holed up in a shack on the
edge of town.'

'Sure. Count me in.' Swain drew a pistol out the waist-
band of his pants and checked it. 'Do you want Danny
Pierce and Will Eldon along?'

'Yeah. Fetch them along to the law office and wait for
me there. I'll check on the sheriff at the doc's before I do
anything else.'

He left the saloon and went back along the street to the
doctor's house. There was a light in the front window. Cole
tried the door, found it unlocked, and entered. When he

64

called for the doctor, Carmody opened a door on the left and stuck his head out. Carmody nodded.

'Come on in, Cole,' he said. 'I've just finished with the sheriff. It'll be touch and go for a few days, but, barring complications, he should make it. My wife will nurse him. I'd better get a move on and ride out to Big G. There just doesn't seem to be enough time to breathe right now.'

'It's good news about the sheriff.' Cole sighed with relief. 'I thought he was done for. I'm on my way now to pick up the men who did the shooting.'

'That's quick work! Who are they?'

'I'll keep that to myself for now. If you hear shooting before you leave town then drop into the law office in case you're needed. But I hope to handle this without gun play.'

'Good luck.' Carmody followed Cole to the front door.

Cole returned to the law office to find Swain, Pierce and Eldon waiting for him. All three were armed. Cole checked his pistol, then eased the weapon back into its holster.

'No shooting unless they start it,' he advised. 'I want them alive to find out what is going on. Two of the men we're after roughed up the sheriff earlier and I think they were joined by a third man when they attacked the law office and wounded the sheriff.'

'They have to be strangers,' said Swain. 'Nobody local would do that. Where are they now?'

'In a shack on the edge of town, and they are strangers, but the third man ain't. He's Floyd Kennedy.'

'Hell! That puts a different face on it!' ejaculated Swain. 'Are you sure Floyd is involved? No one has seen him back from prison yet, and I can't believe he's mixed up in more trouble already. And why would he wanta shoot the sheriff?'

'That's what I need to ask him.' Cole shrugged. 'Let's pick him up, and then we'll ask him.'

They walked along the street to the edge of town, their boots making no sound in the dust. A light showed here and there in windows of the huddle of shacks but there was complete silence. Cole led the way to the building Jane Kennedy had visited earlier and paused in the shadows. Lantern light showed at the window. He motioned for the three posse men to remain silent. They drew their pistols and waited stolidly – experienced posse men. Cole approached the window beside the door and peered through a small tear in the sacking which was being used as a curtain. All he could see was a corner of a table, and the blue shirt of one of the men who had roughed up the sheriff He listened intently but heard nothing from inside the ramshackle building.

Cole stepped in front of the door and tried it silently. It did not budge, and he guessed that a solid wooden bar would be in place on the inside. It would be useless trying to batter a way in quickly. He glanced at Swain, Pierce and Eldon, saw that they were ready to back his play, and knocked on the door. For a moment there was no reaction, and then a harsh voice called from within.

'Who in hell is out there?'

'Jane Kennedy asked me to drop by with a message for her brother Floyd,' Cole replied. 'Have I got the right shack?'

'No. I ain't heard of Jane Kennedy or her brother,' was the swift reply.

'Jane said her brother would play it smart but that I

66

should insist on seeing him,' Cole continued. 'The message is urgent, so he'd better show himself.'

A silence followed, then Cole heard the sound of a bar being raised on the inside of the door. He drew his pistol and prepared for action. The door opened slowly and a face peered out as the muzzle of a pistol poked around the edge of the door to cover him. Cole reached out with his left hand and clamped his fingers around the barrel of the pistol, forcing it out of line with his body, and then lunged forward and hit the door with his chest, crashing it open.

The man uttered a cry and fell back. Cole followed closely and entered the shack, moving to his left. He levelled his pistol as he glanced quickly around the big room. The man wearing the green shirt was rolling on the floor. The blue-shirted man was in the act of springing up from his seat at the table, his right hand clawing for his holstered gun. There was no sign of Floyd Kennedy.

Cole squeezed off a shot at the blue shirt. The shack reverberated to the crash and gun smoke spouted. The bullet thudded into the right shoulder of the hardcase and his gun blasted instantly but the muzzle was pointing downward and the slug tore a long strip of wood out of the table top. The hardcase sprawled face down on the table, dropping his gun, and then rolled limply to the floor.

Swain and Pierce came into the shack with drawn guns. Eldon moved into the doorway, his gun ready. The hardcase wearing the green shirt was scrabbling for his pistol on the floor, but gave up when he realized that he was outnumbered. Cole picked up the gun dropped by the injured hardcase. Swain dragged the other man to his feet and searched him. Cole heaved a sigh, wondering what had happened to Floyd Kennedy.

'OK,' he said. 'Let's take 'em to the jail and then we'll hear what they've got to say for themselves. Swain, I need to take a posse out to Big G. Lance Clifford was shot this afternoon and there was other trouble on the range. I'll need someone to take care of the law office while I'm away, and I hope to put a stop to whatever is going on.'

'I'll take over the law office,' said Eldon.

They removed the prisoners from the shack and went back to the office. Cole was well pleased with the way the situation was turning in his favour, but he was concerned about Mart, and hoped his brother was following orders out at Big G.

FIVE

Buck Kennedy headed fast for BK, his thoughts tumbling through his mind like white water in a flash flood. It felt good to be hitting back at those he suspected of being his enemies. He had sat back while Floyd was in jail, taking the shame of it on the chin, biding his time while his enemies got stronger. But the waiting was over. Floyd was on his way back to home range, and the trouble should be done with by the time his son showed up at the ranch. He used all his strength to fight the stallion, and raked its flanks with his spurs, forcing it to gallop in a wild charge for the distant BK.

His mind was teeming as he rode. When he thought of Frank Bartram, the hotel owner, a thrill of satisfaction darted through him because he had finally solved the problem of Bartram's big mouth. Two Winchester slugs had taken care of it; he wished he had killed the son of a bitch years ago! The murder had bolstered his determination, and now he felt ready for anything. He was through waiting. He had spent years living on a knife edge of uncertainty, afraid that word would get out of his dissolute, criminal youth, when everything had happened,

69

from bank robbery to murder. Now he had started cleaning up he was going to wipe the slate clean. He would hit the county like a tornado, and when the smoke cleared and his former saddle pards were dead, all his troubles would be over.

He knew he had to get rid of the Paston brothers, for the first thing Floyd would want to do when he returned was to settle his account with Mart Paston, which would mean a return to prison for Floyd. Kennedy pulled his horse down to a canter, fighting the animal for mastery and having to use brute strength to control it. He was aware that he had to keep hitting his enemies without respite, and, acting on an impulse, he turned the horse in the direction of the Big G ranch. He needed to see if Carney and Quirk had caught up with Mart Paston and Lance Gifford, for the sooner those two were dead the better he would feel. Then he would concentrate on the sheriff and shut him up permanently, before Horden could open his mouth about that bank raid of thirty years ago. Then, with Horden dead, there would remain only one other man who had participated in that robbery – Bob Liffen, who owned the bank in Squaw Creek.

He shook his head as he held the stallion under control. There was no end to the trouble arising from that long-past incident. But he was aware that he carried the cure for it in his holster, and sensed it was time to snuff out all opposition. Horden had said that Liffen was making disagreeable noises about the past, so he would confront Liffen when he had taken care of the Paston brothers.

He passed the Lazy P ranch, which looked deserted, and was impatient for Floyd to take it over. He wondered if his boy was out of jail yet. He had not received word from Floyd, and hoped the youngster would toe the line when he showed up. He headed for Big G, and soon picked up tracks heading in the same direction. He noted the prints left by Cole and Mart Paston's horses, and then spotted two more sets of tracks following them, which he assumed were left by the mounts of Carney and Quirk.

When he came upon the bodies of Carney and Quirk, stiffening in death in the hot sunshine, he reined up to stare at them in disbelief. What the hell had happened? It looked like Cole Paston was proving too tough to kill: he realized that he would have to do the killing himself if he wanted it done at all. He rode on, letting the stallion run at its own pace, and when he spotted Mart Paston in the distance, sitting on a knoll with a couple of horses grazing nearby, he rode into cover and changed direction to sneak in closer, unseen.

Kennedy eased into a gully and dismounted. He left the stallion tied to a stunted tree and pulled his Winchester from its saddle boot. He followed the gully until he was within a hundred yards of the knoll where Mart Paston was sitting, and was able to see Lance Gifford stretched out on the grass. He also saw a buckboard approaching from the direction of the BG ranch, and crouched in cover to wait and watch.

Hank Gifford was riding behind the buckboard, accompanied by two of his crew, and they were alert; ready for trouble. Kennedy heaved a sigh. He needed more action to assuage his impatience. The three long years of waiting for Floyd to get out of prison had taken its toll of his nerves and he was ready to explode, but he had enough sense to be cautious. He wanted Hank and Lance Gifford dead, but there were other men in the county who were more dangerous to his way of life.

Kennedy watched Lance Gifford being placed in the buckboard on a pile of straw. Hank Gifford tied his horse behind the wagon and got in with his son. Mart Paston rode with the two Big G riders and the party headed back to the Gifford ranch. Kennedy was tempted to toss lead at them, but resisted the impulse. His turn would come. He went back for his stallion and followed the buckboard at a distance, careful to stay out of sight.

Daylight was fading when he rode into a thicket and dismounted. He hoped that Mart Paston would make the mistake of returning alone to Lazy P. Shadows lengthened across the range. The blue of the sky darkened imperceptibly. Stars began to show in the great overhead. Lights illuminated the windows of the ranch house and bunkhouse. Kennedy waited patiently, his thoughts turning over ceaselessly. It was almost full dark when he saw a figure emerge from the ranch house and swing into the saddle of a horse tethered to a porch post. He waited stoically, fighting his impatience, and watched the rider approaching. When he was able to recognize Mart Paston, a thrill of anticipation stabbed through his breast. He palmed his pistol and cocked it.

Mart pushed his horse into a lope and headed towards the Lazy P. He did not see Buck Kennedy's big figure crouched in cover, and set himself for the long ride back to his home ranch. When he saw the ears of his horse flick to the right he glanced in that direction, aware that the animal had spotted something or someone. He caught a glimpse of a black figure rising up out of cover and snatched at the butt of his holstered pistol.

The flash of a shot split the even shade of starlit night.

Orange flame stabbed towards Mart. The crash of the shot battered the silence. Mart felt the lightning flash of a slug smashing into his left side, and it was as if the night itself had exploded in his face. Pain flared in his body. The impact of the bullet knocked him over sideways. His mount reared in shock and Mart went out of the saddle. He fell to the ground, his left foot becoming trapped in its stirrup, and he was dragged by the horse when it bolted. Then his head struck something solid and his senses fled.

Kennedy froze with uplifted gun, listening intently, his hard gaze fixed on the Big G ranch while he wondered if the shot had been heard. He watched for movement as gun echoes faded away. When he was satisfied that the shooting had not been heard he fetched his stallion and rode out to where Mart Paston's horse had halted. The animal was grazing now, with Mart's left foot still trapped in the stirrup. Kennedy cocked his gun and aimed at the motionless figure. He needed to ensure that his victim was dead. His finger was trembling on the trigger when he caught the sound of approaching hoofs coming from the direction of Squaw Creek. He holstered his gun quickly and swung the stallion back into cover.

He was lost in the shadows before a rider appeared and halted beside Mart Paston's horse. He heard an exclamation of shock and saw the newcomer dismount. A match scraped, flared, and was held close to Mart's face. Then the newcomer climbed back into his saddle and galloped into the Big G yard. Kennedy could hear the rider calling an alarm as he hammered across the ranch yard.

Kennedy turned away and remounted the stallion. He

set it into motion and rode fast along the trail to town. He could always finish off Mart Paston, if he was not already dead.

Mart was not fully conscious; aware only of a terrible pain in the region of his left hip. He heard the sound of Kennedy passing on his way to town and alarm brought him fully to his senses. He discovered that he was lying on his back, and gazed up at the starry sky. He raised his head slightly and looked for the horse he could hear passing close by. He saw the rider in silhouette but could not identify him. The horse was of a pale colour. Then he heard the rider cursing the restive animal, and recognized Buck Kennedy's voice.

Mart slumped then, his senses receding, but he clung to an edge of consciousness and felt for his pistol. His trembling fingers warned that his holster was empty, and he recalled having drawn the weapon before he was shot. The sound of Kennedy's passing faded and silence returned. He pressed his hand against his left side and felt the spreading stickiness of oozing blood.

When he tried to move he realized that his left foot was still caught in the stirrup, and as he tried to free himself his horse moved nervously. He soothed the animal, which resumed its grazing, but Mart was unable to get his foot loose. He relaxed, and minutes later the sound of approaching hoofbeats alerted him, this time coming from the direction of the Gifford ranch.

A rider reined up beside him, and Hank Gifford called his name. There was a thump of boots on grass as the rancher sprang from his saddle. Then Gifford was bending over him.

'What happened, Mart?' Gifford demanded. 'Joe

Santos spotted you as he came to the ranch. Are you bad hurt?'

'It was Buck Kennedy,' Mart said. 'I heard him cursing his horse as he rode away. He shot me from cover. I'm hit in the body, Hank, and it feels bad.'

'The wagon is coming,' Gifford said. 'Take it easy, Mart. We'll get you back to the ranch. I hope Cole has told the doc to come on out here. Lance ain't so good, and now you.'

'Get me on my feet, Hank,' Mart said. 'If I can climb back into my saddle I'll go after Buck Kennedy. He won't get away with this.'

'You just take it easy,' Gifford said in a soothing tone. 'There'll be plenty of time later to get Kennedy. I expect Cole will show up with a posse when Doc comes.'

Mart relaxed and closed his eyes. His senses receded, but the pain in his left side kept unconsciousness at bay. He heard the sound of wagon wheels grating on the hard ground, and minutes later he was lifted and placed in the back of a buckboard. He lost consciousness then. When he regained his senses once more he was lying on a couch in the big room at the ranch with the ranch cook bending over him. Hank Gifford was standing in the background, an expression of deep concern on his rugged face.

'It looks nasty, Mart,' Gifford observed, 'but you're still breathing so I reckon you'll do. The slug hit your left hip bone and turned outwards instead of going through your belly. Cookie will patch you up good. He's already stopped the bleeding, and you'll be OK until the doc gets here.'

'Thanks, Hank. I'm obliged to you.' Mart closed his eyes and slipped back into unconsciousness.

He knew nothing more until pain dragged him back to

his senses. He opened his eyes to find Doc Carmody bending over him.

'It's OK Mart; lie still while I examine you,' Carmody said. 'I would have been out here a lot sooner but there was trouble in town before I left and my services were required.'

'What happened in town, Doc?' Hank Gifford demanded.

'What didn't happen?' Carmody countered. 'Hell, I don't really know where to start! The sheriff was beaten up in a saloon by two strangers. Then Cole Paston rode in with Buster Askew as his prisoner. After that the law office was shot up, and the sheriff was hit by a slug. He is pretty badly hurt, but I think he'll make it. When I rode out to come here, Cole was about to arrest the two men who beat up the sheriff. I sure wish I knew what is going on.'

'Buck Kennedy has gone on the warpath,' said Gifford. 'He ambushed Mart and was heading for town the last Mart saw of him. Apart from that, some of Kennedy's outfit shot my boy Lance.'

'I didn't see Kennedy on the trail,' Carmody said. He shrugged. 'Perhaps that was just as well, huh? I'd better check on Lance now. I want to head back to town soon as I can in case there was more shooting after I left.' He patted Mart's shoulder. 'I'll get back to you shortly, son. You'll be OK.'

Mart tried to sit up but the pain in his hip area nailed him down. 'I ought to get to town,' he said, stifling a groan. 'Cole may need help.'

'You ain't going anywhere,' Carmody replied. 'Just lie still and give yourself time to recover. You couldn't help Cole or anybody else in your present state.'

Mart gave up then, relaxed and closed his eyes. He wondered about his brother as he tried to rest, and eventually fell into an uneasy sleep.

Cole was relieved when he slammed a cell door on his two prisoners. They were tough-looking men, and he was eager to question them. He examined the hardcase who had been shot and discovered that his wound was not serious.

'He'll have to wait until the doctor gets back,' Cole said. 'Charlie, can you do something about the broken window? I feel kind of naked in here with the glass gone.'

'I could put shutters up for tonight,' Swain replied. 'Will that do?'

'It'll have to.' Cole nodded. 'Danny, give Charlie a hand. Will can remain here and help me with questioning the prisoners. Let's have the uninjured one in the front office, Will, and I'll get on with it.'

Swain and Pierce departed. Eldon drew his pistol as he entered the cell block. He escorted the uninjured hardcase back into the office. Cole went behind the desk and sat down. His prisoner stared at the floor, his expression sullen.

'You're in a lot of trouble, friend,' Cole said without preamble. 'You rode into town, assaulted the sheriff, and then joined up with an ex-convict to shoot up this office. The sheriff was hit by one of your slugs, and the doc reckons he may live. But if he dies then there'll be a murder charge against those who took part in the shooting, so whichever way you look at it, you're in a lot of trouble, and it'll be in your best interests to tell me what this is all about.'

'You've got the wrong men,' the hardcase replied. 'Me

and my pard are riding the grubline. We stopped at the BK ranch earlier and had some food, then came to town for a drink. We plan to move on tomorrow. We didn't get into any trouble. We're just a couple of cowhands looking for work.'

'What's your name?' asked Cole. He paused and waited for a reply but the man shook his head. Cole suppressed a sigh as he tried to contain his impatience. 'If you say you've caused no trouble around here then you'll give me your name,' he continued. 'You're not acting like an innocent man. But then you're not innocent, are you? I can establish that. I have a reliable witness who can identify the two men who beat up the sheriff, and he can be in here in a couple of minutes.'

The hardcase shrugged. 'I'm Al Lockton, and my pard is Jim Sawyer, if you must know. Why are you asking all these questions?' he demanded.

'Where has Floyd Kennedy gone?' Cole asked.

'I've never heard of Floyd Kennedy.'

'He was in that shack with you some minutes ago.' Cole smiled. 'I followed Floyd's sister Jane to the shack and watched her talking to Floyd before she left. Floyd saw her off. He's just got out of prison, so where did you meet up with him? Were you in the pen along with him?'

'I've never been in prison. Like I said; it must be two other men you're after.'

'Bill,' Cole said, 'take a walk along to the saloon and tell Joe Brady I wanta see him. He witnessed the attack on the sheriff earlier and can recognize the men who did it.'

Eldon departed. Cole watched his prisoner, who sat motionless and sullen, his gaze fixed on the floor under the desk. Silence held sway until Eldon returned with Joe Brady.

'Yeah,' Brady said without hesitation. 'He's one of the two men who beat up the sheriff. This one did the beating while the other guy held a gun on the sheriff.'

'Thanks, Joe,' said Cole. 'Look at the man in the cells and see if you recognize him.'

Eldon escorted Brady into the cell block, and they returned instantly.

'You've got the right pair,' Brady said. 'You want I should sign a statement to that effect?'

'Not right now, Joe. I'll let you know when I get to that stage. Thanks for your help.'

'It was a real pleasure,' said Brady, and departed.

Cole glanced at Eldon. 'Lock him up, Will,' he instructed. 'It looks like I'll have to do this the hard way. I'll have to go through the town, and with any luck I'll find Floyd Kennedy. You'll be OK here on your own until Charlie and Danny get back, huh?'

'Sure. No sweat. You go and do what's needed.'

Cole waited until Al Lockton had been returned to his cell, then left the office. He paused on the boardwalk and looked around the shadowed town, mulling over what had occurred. He really needed to pick up Floyd Kennedy, and he wondered if the ex-convict had left town. He walked back to the shack where he had arrested the two hardcases and checked at the back for the horses that had been there on his first visit. One of the animals was gone, and he guessed it was Floyd's mount.

He went back along the street to the Ellard house and knocked at the front door, which was opened by Sam Ellard, the freight-line owner.

'Howdy. Cole, what brings you here at this time of the night?' Ellard was tall and thin, like two boards clapped together. His face was long, angular; his eyes brown, deeply set under thick black brows.

'I saw Jane Kennedy come in here a short while ago, Sam,' Cole said. 'Is she still here?'

'I don't think so. Hold on and I'll check. Step inside for a couple of minutes.'

Cole entered the house and closed the door. Ellard went through to a back room and returned with his daughter Polly at his heels.

'Hello, Cole,' said Polly. She was tall and thin, with an attractive, oval face. She smiled in a friendly fashion and Cole reciprocated. He had always had a soft spot for Polly. 'Pa said you're looking for Jane. She was here but only to say she couldn't stay. She left immediately, saying she was heading back to BK. I'm sorry you've missed her.'

'Thanks, Polly. I'll catch up with her another time.' Cole turned to the door.

'She hasn't been getting into trouble again with that temper of hers, has she, Cole?' Sam Ellard demanded.

'No, it's nothing like that. I'm wondering if she knows where her brother Floyd has got to. He was in town earlier, but seems to have disappeared.'

'I knew it,' Ellard declared. 'I heard about Horden getting roughed up, and then shot. I said to Martha that it had to be Floyd up to his old tricks. The county has been quiet since he was jailed. But all that will change now he's on the prowl again. I hope you can grab him before he causes too much trouble, Cole.'

'I don't know yet that he is involved in anything bad,' said Cole, 'but I shall find out. Sorry I had to bother you.'

'Any time, Cole.' Ellard came forward as Cole departed and closed the door behind him.

Cole paused on the sidewalk and looked around. When he heard the scuff of a leather boot in the shadows to his left he whirled to face the direction from which the sound came, his right hand dropping to the butt of his holstered gun. He halted the movement when he saw a woman's figure and then recognized Jane Kennedy. She came forward out of the shadows and paused before him.

'I need to speak to you, Cole,' she said in a cool tone. 'I wanted to talk to the sheriff but I heard he'd been shot.'

'That's right,' Cole replied. 'Is Floyd back home yet?'

'Yes, I have seen him, and that's what I want to talk to you about. I spoke to him earlier, in a shack on the edge of town, and what he said makes me think he is gonna kill our pa.'

'What?' Cole was astounded. He had expected her to deny seeing her brother, or to send him on a wild-goose chase after Floyd. 'Go on,' he urged. 'What did Floyd say?'

'I don't know what his trouble is, but he's bitter about a lot of things, and I was surprised when he went on about Pa. He made some wild threats against your brother Mart, and Pa, and when I tried to talk him out of it he showed me the door and told me to get lost. That's why I need to talk to you. You've got to find Floyd and stop him before he does something really bad.'

'I reckon anything Floyd said to you was just wild talk,' Cole mused. 'He's been behind bars for three years, and that will have affected him some, but I don't think he'll go off half-cocked and do something stupid. Why don't you give him a few days to settle down? I reckon he'll change his tune when he's had time to think.'

'I heard that Frank Bartram was shot dead in front of his hotel earlier. Floyd made threats against Bartram, and

I think Bartram's death is the first of several that will happen now Floyd is back on the loose. Don't you think you should check him out in case he shot Bartram? It is your job to protect the folks of this county.'

'Sure it is.' Cole suppressed a sigh. 'OK, Jane, I guess I'll get after Floyd and have a talk with him. Where has he gone, do you know?'

'Back to BK. I'm riding out there myself, so get your horse and come along. You'd never forgive yourself if you let this chance go by and then Floyd killed someone.'

'I don't know if I can leave town right now.' Cole shook his head. 'I've got three prisoners in the jail that I need to get statements from. With the sheriff shot up I'm on my own, and I can't be in two places at once.'

'You can always get statements from prisoners,' Jane urged. 'It's a question of what's more important, isn't it? How will it seem to folks around here if you sit back in your office while Floyd goes on a killing spree? He sounded mighty spiteful to me earlier.'

'OK.' Cole sighed. 'I guess I can't just sit around and hope everything will turn out right. I'll ride with you, but first I have to drop in at the office and tell the men there what I'm gonna do. Walk with me, if you like, and then I'll get my horse from the livery barn.'

He walked in the direction of the law office and Jane fell into step at his side. Cole wondered about the girl, for she had never been friendly towards him. But he supposed that she was concerned about her father. If Floyd was of a mind to settle some old scores then Cole would not be surprised by anything he did.

Charlie Swain was erecting wooden shutters in the front window of the office. Cole explained the situation, and

Swain agreed to take over in town until Cole returned.

'I reckon you should take a couple of posse men along with you if you're gonna brace Floyd,' Swain suggested. 'He ain't likely to come quietly, and the sight of you will be like a red rag to a bull. I'll side you, if you like.'

'I'd rather handle this on my own,' Cole replied. 'I don't want to push Floyd into anything. All I want is a quiet chat with him.'

'Are you talking about the same Floyd I'm thinking of?' Swain laughed. 'If you'll take my advice you'll get the drop on Floyd and bring him back in irons. But I guess you know your business best, so good luck. I'll see you when you get back – if you ever do.'

Cole turned away. He would not take any chances with Floyd Kennedy. Jane accompanied him silently.

'You know how folks think about Floyd,' Cole said presently. 'Most men around here wouldn't give him a dog's chance if the chips went down. Where is your horse, Jane?'

'It's in the livery barn. Let's hurry it up and get moving, huh?'

They continued in silence, and Cole remained alert, aware of the enmity that existed between him and the Kennedy family. When they approached the front door of the livery barn, Cole stepped aside for Jane to precede him. She passed through the circle of light from the overhead lantern and walked to the right. Cole attempted to skirt the yellow glare but was compelled to pass through it, and his muscles tensed as he was highlighted.

He hurried forward with the intention of fading quickly into the surrounding darkness, his right hand dropping instinctively to the butt of his holstered pistol. The interior of the barn was gloomy, and he could hear Jane moving in a stall to his right. A horse stamped and Jane's voice sounded, low and soothing. Cole went into the shadows, aware that he was still silhouetted against the light. He could barely see. He narrowed his eyes and tried to pierce the surrounding shadows. A movement to his right had him pulling his gun, but it was only half-drawn when the barrel of a pistol crashed against his head.

Cole dropped to his knees. He dragged his Colt out and lifted it, but a second blow smacked him heavily on the right temple before he could cock the weapon. A cascade of coloured lights flared inside his skull, and he felt no pain as he fell forward on to his face. . . .

SIX

It was before midnight when Buck Kennedy rode into the main street of Squaw Creek. He was sweating with a passion that had increased on his long ride, and although he was pleased with what he had accomplished during the day, he was keenly aware that some loose ends of his past life needed close attention. He dismounted outside Brady's saloon, tied the stallion to an awning post, and paused on the boardwalk to look around the shadowed street. The town was quiet, and he wondered what the townsfolk had made of Frank Bartram's murder. His lips twitched into a grim smile as he thrust open the batwings and strode into the saloon.

If he could kill Cole Paston now, he would be happy, he thought. His eyes narrowed as he looked around. Brady was talking with the 'tender, and there were a couple of men bellied up to the bar, drinking beer. Four men sat at a table across the saloon, playing poker. The lamplight was glaring, and painted the faces of those present with a deathlike shade of pale yellow.

Brady came to where Kennedy was standing when the rancher slammed a big hand on the bar.

'What'll you have, Buck?' Brady demanded.

'Whiskey,' Kennedy replied.

Brady poured whiskey into a glass and then set it in front of Kennedy. 'It's been a real humdinger today.' He observed. 'Your boy was in town – the first time in three years, and there's been hell to pay. Someone put two slugs into Frank Bartram while he was sitting in the doorway of the hotel this afternoon – killed him stone dead! Then Horden was roughed up by a couple of hardcase strangers – right in here, it happened! After that, the law office was attacked and Horden was shot.'

'The hell you say!' Kennedy was staggered by the news. He gulped down his whiskey. 'Is Horden dead?'

'No. He's hanging on. Doc reckons he's got a chance of pulling through. Say, Cole Paston rode in earlier with Buster Askew under arrest. I reckon that's why the jail was attacked.'

'And you think Floyd had something to do with the trouble?' Kennedy asked.

'Nobody knows.' Brady shook his head. 'But things like that happen when Floyd is around, huh? It's been real quiet in the county while your boy was in prison.'

'Have you any idea where Floyd is right now?'

'I ain't seen him. But I can tell you that Cole Paston is looking for him.'

Kennedy headed for the door, paused, and looked back at Brady before saying, 'If Floyd does come in then tell him to wait here for me, huh?'

'Sure thing, Buck,' Brady replied.

Kennedy left his horse tied to the post outside and walked to the law office. There was no light shining in the window, and when he drew nearer he saw shutters in place. He tried the door of the office, discovered it was locked, and hammered on it with a heavy fist.

'Who is it?' a voice demanded from inside.

'Buck Kennedy. I need to talk to Cole Paston. Open the door, damn you!'

'Cole ain't here right now. Come back in the morning. He should be back by then.'

'Who in hell is inside this office?' Kennedy demanded in a rising tone.

'Go to hell.'

Kennedy stepped back a pace, raised his right leg, and kicked at the door with all his strength and weight. The door flew inward and struck Charlie Swain, knocking him to the floor. Swain rolled over and got to his hands and knees. He looked up at Kennedy, and saw a pistol in the rancher's hand, cocked and ready for action.

'You're making a big mistake,' Swain said as he regained his feet. He was careful to keep his hand away from the butt of his holstered pistol.

'Where is Cole Paston?' Kennedy demanded.

'Gone out to Big G.' Swain shrugged. 'There's been trouble on the range, and some of your outfit is mixed up in it. Lance Gifford was shot by Buster Askew, so Cole arrested Askew.'

'I want to see Buster.'

'No can do!' Swain shook his head. 'Cole gave orders that no one is to see Askew before he's made a statement.'

Kennedy cocked his gun and aimed it at Swain's heart. 'Do like I say or you're dead, Swain,' he rasped. 'Get the cell keys and open the doors.'

Swain looked into the black muzzle of Kennedy's gun and realized that the rancher was deadly serious. He shrugged, turned to the desk, and picked up the bunch of cell keys.

'I'm only the hired help around here,' Swain said. 'I ain't gonna get myself shot for a creep like Askew. If you want him out then you can have him, but be ready to take it up with Cole when he comes looking for you.'

'You've got a lot of sense.' Kennedy grinned. 'OK. Get rid of your gun.'

Swain tossed his pistol into a corner, picked up the cell keys, and went into the cell block with Kennedy following closely. Askew was lying on the bunk in a cell, and sprang to his feet when Swain approached. He grinned when he saw Kennedy.

'You sure took your time, boss,' Askew observed. 'What the hell has been going on?'

Swain unlocked the cell door. Askew emerged, his right fist swinging. He clipped Swain on the jaw and the posse man went down heavily.

'Drag him into the cell and lock him in,' Kennedy said. 'I heard that Floyd is in town and I need to find him quick.'

'Have you heard what's been going on around here since you were in town earlier?' demanded Askew.

'Do you know where Floyd is right now?' Kennedy countered.

'I don't even know if he is back on home range,' Askew replied, shrugging his wide shoulders. His thick lips were pulled tightly against his teeth. 'The hell if I know what is going on. I set out to handle a simple gun chore earlier, and then everything went haywire. If you know what is happening then you better tell me about it, boss.'

'Let's get out of here and then we'll talk,' Kennedy

replied. He could see Swain in the cell, listening intently, and he stepped close to the barred door to confront the discomfited posse man. 'You can tell Cole Paston that he'd better leave the county if he wants to stay healthy. I'm paying any debts Floyd left behind when he went to prison.'

Swain turned away and sat down heavily on the bunk in the cell. Kennedy watched him for a moment, then swung away and headed for the front office, followed by Askew, who found his gun belt and buckled it around his waist. His pistol was missing and he saw it lying on the desk. He checked the weapon before thrusting it into its holster.

'I'm ready to go,' Askew said. 'You want me to hunt up Carney and Quirk to finish off that chore we were handling?'

'You'll have a long way to ride to catch up with that pair,' Kennedy rasped. He gave a brief account of what happened on the range after Askew had been arrested. 'You can ride out to the Gifford spread and look around after sunup for any sign of Mart Paston lying around dead, which he should be because I put a slug in him. It'll be daylight by the time you get out there, and if you don't see Paston around then wait your chance and put a slug through Hank Gifford soon as you can. Cole Paston rode out that way, so I heard, and if you can kill him as well then so much the better. I've got things to do around town, and I'll ride back to BK when I get through here.'

'Sure, boss.' Askew went to the street door. He glanced over his shoulder at Kennedy, gauged the rancher's mood, and compressed his lips. 'See you later,' he said.

Kennedy remained in the office until Askew had departed, thinking about his next move. When he departed he walked to the huddle of private houses standing in a small square beyond the bank, where the residences of the businessmen of the town were located. He saw a light in the front window of Bob Liffen's house despite the lateness of the hour, and he approached silently. When he rapped on the banker's front door the curtain covering the big front window was twitched aside and Liffen peered out into the shadows. He recognized Kennedy's big figure, lifted a hand in acknowledgement, and dropped the curtain. A moment later the front door was opened.

'What are you doing in town at this time of the night, Buck?' Liffen demanded. He was tall and broad-shouldered; a powerful man with an abrupt manner. 'Is your presence connected with the trouble that's been going on around here since this afternoon? Have you heard that Frank Bartram was gunned down in his own doorway?'

'Frank died because he ran off at the mouth once too often.' Kennedy heaved a sigh. 'Ain't you gonna ask me in? I need to talk to you before I head back to BK.'

Liffen stepped back out of the doorway and Kennedy entered the house. He could smell whiskey on the banker's breath as Liffen closed the door.

'I heard that Floyd is back in town,' Liffen said. 'Is he to blame for all this trouble?'

'I don't think so.' Kennedy smiled. His eyes were narrowed, cold, filled with deadly intention. 'I'm back of it. I've been paying some debts that are long overdue.'

'So it was you killed Bartram!' Liffen heaved a sigh of relief. 'I was wondering when you were going to stop his mouth. I've heard talk around town about the Mulejaw bank raid. Someone is raking over old coals and raising smoke. It must have been you that killed Mike Paston because he kept harping on about Mulejaw.'

'Yeah, I put him down because of his big mouth. And I've heard that you've been talking out of turn, and that won't do, Bob. The past should be left alone. Even Horden sometimes ran off at the lip. I've heard that he mentioned those old days, especially after a night's drinking.'

'Did you shoot Pete as well?' Liffen demanded.

'No. Someone beat me to it. But it was in my mind to put him down. We can't afford to have questions asked about Mulejaw.'

'I've always suspected that you killed Mike Paston to shut him up.' Liffen spoke in a stilted tone. 'Is that why you wanted to see me? Are you figuring to shut my mouth?'

'If Horden pegs out, we'll be the only two left out of the old gang.' Kennedy shook his head.

'I reckon we should drink to the old days,' Liffen turned to an inner door. 'Come on in and we'll chew the fat.'

Kennedy followed the banker into an inner room, and paused on the threshold when he saw Porter, the new bank guard, seated at a table. A whiskey bottle and some glasses were on a tray, and two hands of cards were lying face down on the table.

'Have I interrupted a game?' Kennedy demanded.

'This is Len Porter, my new guard at the bank,' Liffen introduced. 'He's living here for a spell.'

'I saw him earlier,' Kennedy said. 'He passed on the message that you wanted to see me. How are you doing, Porter?'

'I'm fine, Mr Kennedy.' Porter eased his chair a few inches back from the desk and leaned back. He was wearing a brown suit, and a bulge showed at his left armpit. He folded his arms, his right hand close to the left lapel of his jacket. His pale eyes were unblinking and he did not take his gaze off Kennedy. The expression on his craggy face hinted at an inner eagerness, as if he were hungry and his next meal had just walked into the room.

'So you're running scared, Bob,' Kennedy observed. 'What's got you going?'

'I'm not scared,' Liffen replied. 'I'm just being careful. Too many of my old friends are going down in the dust.'

'You've got nothing to worry about if you keep your mouth shut,' Kennedy said. 'You've got as much to lose as I have, Bob; perhaps more. It's taken us a long time to get where we are today, and I don't want to start losing out at this late stage. We've both worked hard for what we've got.'

'So what's on your mind, Buck?' Liffen sat down on a chair behind the table and looked up at Kennedy. His rugged face was expressionless, but there was a glint in his pale eyes. His hands were resting palms down on the table, and the long fingers of his right hand tapped silently on the green tablecloth.

'You sent a message that you wanted to see me,' Kennedy countered. 'So what's gnawing at you?'

'I wanted to clear the air between us.' Liffen sighed. 'Whatever is going on around here, I want you to know that it is none of my doing. I think someone not connected to us in the old days is trying to uncover what happened at Mulejaw, and your guess is as good as mine about that. You killed Mike Paston and Frank Bartram because you figured they were talking, but it could be someone we don't know who is trying to force the pace – someone who has heard the rumours and has managed to put two and two together.'

'You got any ideas on that?' Kennedy demanded.

'Hell no!' Liffen shook his head emphatically. 'I was hoping you might have some idea. I'm worried as hell. If Horden dies then there are only two of us left, and you're the one who is shooting first. All I want to do is make my position clear to you.'

'You've got as much to lose as I have,' Kennedy said. 'I guess that puts you in the clear, Bob, so quit worrying. You don't need a gun guard to protect you from me.'

'Just so long as we know where we stand, Buck. So what will you do now?'

'I need to find out how Horden is doing, and then I want to find Floyd and put him straight about certain things.'

'What about Horden?' Liffen asked.

'What about him?'

'I think he should die.' Liffen shrugged. 'Like you said, we've both got a lot to lose, and Horden is loose-lipped about the old days.'

'I'll hold my hand to see what happens over the next day or so.' Kennedy half-turned to the door, but paused. 'With any luck, Horden will die from his wound, but if he doesn't then I'll attend to him.'

'Don't take anything at face value,' Liffen warned. 'I've got a hunch that bad trouble is coming up for us, and if we don't cotton on to it before it strikes then we'll lose out.'

'Who can cause trouble for us? It would have to be someone from thirty years ago, and all those men are dead now.'

'But one of them could have talked about Mulejaw before he died,' Liffen insisted.

'So why has it taken so long for the truth to start coming out?' Kennedy shook his head. 'I think you're wrong, Bob.'

'Then why did Bartram try to shoot it out with Mart Paston three years ago? Mike Paston was the father of Cole and Mart. Perhaps Mike said something to his two sons.'

'You're digging deep,' Kennedy mused. 'I reckon if Mart or Cole Paston knew anything about the past it would have blown up in our faces before now – likewise if either of them learned I'd killed their father. Leave it lie for a bit and we'll see what comes up.'

Liffen nodded, but his expression showed doubt. Kennedy turned away and departed.

Liffen remained motionless until he heard the front door slam behind Kennedy.

'You better get after him, Porter, and see what he does next. If it looks like he's going to kill Horden then stop him. I think I need the sheriff on my side.'

'Do you want me to kill Kennedy?' Porter demanded. 'Lay it on the line, Mr Liffen. I like clear-cut orders. That way I won't have any hesitation.'

'If he goes after Horden then you must kill him,' Liffen said. 'You can see the kind of man Buck Kennedy is, and he's got blood in his eye. He's admitted killing Frank Bartram and Mike Paston. Now Horden's life is on the line, and while I wouldn't want the sheriff to start spouting about things that happened years ago, I suspect that if Kennedy kills him then I'll be next in line for the chop.'

Porter got to his feet and made for the door. 'I'll report back to you first thing in the morning,' he said.

'Unless you have to kill Kennedy tonight,' Liffen said. 'If that happens then I shall want to know immediately.'

Porter nodded and departed.

Kennedy went back to the main street and stood in the shadows while he looked around. He saw a light in the front window of Doc Carmody's house and went towards it. The light was in the doctor's office, and a blind was pulled down on the inside of the window. Kennedy saw a shadow cross the room and recognized Sue Carmody, the doctor's wife. He went to the front door and rapped loudly. A moment later, Mrs Carmody, a tall, slender woman, opened the door and peered out.

'Oh, it's you, Mr Kennedy,' she said. 'If you want the doctor then I'm afraid you're out of luck. He was called out to Big G earlier, and I don't expect him back before morning.'

'I heard there was trouble at the Gifford place,' Kennedy said. 'I'm concerned about the sheriff. I wouldn't have called at this time but I saw you moving around in the office so I guess you're taking care of Horden. How is he doing?'

'He's holding his own at the moment, but the critical time has yet to come. He's feverish, and until that breaks we won't know how he'll come out of it.'

'Does anyone know what happened to him? It's a bad business when the sheriff ain't safe in his own office.'

'I don't know the circumstances of the shooting. Cole Paston was in the office, or just leaving it, I believe, and he found no trace of the men who did the shooting.'

'I'll drop by again in the morning.' Kennedy turned away as Sue Carmody closed the front door.

Kennedy considered for a moment. Horden would

keep for another day, he decided. Now he needed to find Floyd. It was too bad his son had come to town before getting in touch with him at BK, but the youngster probably had his own reasons for wasting no time settling his affairs.

A faint movement in the shadows attracted Kennedy's attention and he became alert, his hand dropping to the butt of his pistol. He caught a glimpse of an indistinct figure standing in a doorway, and a straying beam of light from a lantern in front of the saloon glinted on a drawn gun.

'Who's there?' Kennedy called. He eased his gun out of leather as he spoke, and covered the figure.

Expecting a reply, he waited tensely, and was shocked when a gun blasted and a long tongue of muzzle flame stabbed at him out of the shadows. The hammering report threw a string of echoes across the street. Kennedy staggered when a blow like a thunderbolt struck him in the left shoulder. He fell back against the wall of a house and then pitched forward on to his face on the hard ground. Pain flared through his body and he jerked convulsively. But he did not lose consciousness, and struggled to concentrate on his gun. He thrust his right hand forward and fired at the figure that came out of the shadows to confront him. His gun blasted twice before his strength failed, and then his head dropped forward and his face smacked solidly against the boardwalk.

Len Porter, the new bank guard, took both Kennedy's desperate shots in the chest. He fell dead as Mrs Carmody emerged from her house and started calling for help. Her cries brought Kennedy back to his senses and he struggled to sit up, biting his bottom lip against the pain in his shoulder. He got to his feet and staggered to where his assailant was stretched out in the dust, and dim light from a nearby lamp gave him a glimpse of the face upturned to the stars. It was Len Porter, the bank guard, and he was dead.

Kennedy tottered along the street to where his stallion was tethered, ignoring Mrs Carmody's calls for him to stop. He climbed wearily into his saddle. The stallion bucked, almost throwing him out of leather, but Kennedy turned the animal and headed out of town. His thoughts were ragged as he rode. It looked like Bob Liffen had come down off the fence, so he would have to be taken care of. But not right now. Kennedy headed for the trail to BK. He needed some men to back his play, and when he came back to Squaw Creek he would be holding all the big cards in this bitter game.

SEVEN

The throbbing pain in his head dragged Cole back to his senses. He tried to lift a hand to his forehead and discovered that his wrists were tied behind his back. For a moment he lay with his mind blank, unable to recall what had happened. Then he remembered the stunning blow to his head and the face of Jane Kennedy came to mind. Had Jane struck him? He opened his eyes and gazed at the lantern alight above his head in the doorway of the livery barn, and then saw a figure step into the pool of light. He blinked to bring his gaze into focus, and recognized Jane Kennedy.

'Say, what's going on?' he demanded. 'What are you up to, Jane?'

'I'm waiting for you to regain your senses,' she replied. 'I couldn't get you into your saddle. I've got your horse ready to travel, so climb up on your feet and get mounted.'

When Cole did not move quickly enough for her, she grasped him by a shoulder and hauled him to his feet. Cole staggered as diiziness assailed him, and he leaned on her.

'You're not that badly hurt,' she admonished. 'It was

only a little tap. I thought you had a hard head.'

'I was gonna ride out with you,' he said. 'So why did you hit me?'

'I haven't been quite truthful with you, Cole. Floyd wanted you out of the way, and blood is thicker than water, so I helped him.'

'Where is Floyd? You didn't have to slug me. I want to talk to him.'

'If you'll get up into your saddle I'll take you to where he is,' she said. 'He's waiting out at the old Martin place.'

'You'll have to untie my hands,' he said. 'I can't mount like this.'

'Don't give me any trouble,' she warned, 'unless you want me to hit you again.'

'You're making a lot of trouble for yourself.' Cole shook his head gingerly in an attempt to dislodge the hammering pain in his skull. 'And that'll be nothing to what will come to Floyd if you go along with him. Untie me right now and I'll forget you hit me. You can go on home and I'll get on about my business.'

'No dice. Floyd has had a rough deal from you Pastons. He wants to get his own back now, and I'm gonna help him.'

'What have I ever done against Floyd? He tried to gun down Mart, and that's why he went to prison. It was his fault, and he was lucky Mart didn't shoot him dead.'

'Are you trying to convince me that you don't know why Floyd went after Mart?'

'You'd better believe it. Mart has never mentioned a thing about that fight.'

'And I suppose you don't know why Mart shot Frank Bartram!' Disbelief sounded in Jane's voice. 'Why don't you try and pull the other one!'

'I tell you I have no idea what happened. All that was three years ago. And you should be hoping that Floyd is gonna turn over a new leaf now he's back. He's got a real good chance to make a fresh start, and he'll need all the help he can get. But attacking me like this ain't doing him any favours.'

'You're wasting your breath. I'll help you up into your saddle and we'll get moving.' Jane led Cole's horse beside a bale of straw. 'Get up on that bale and I'll hump you into your saddle.'

'And if I don't?' Cole demanded.

'I'll shoot you and leave you dead,' she replied. 'That's Floyd's orders.'

Cole stared into her eyes and decided that she was deadly serious. He stepped up on to the bale of straw and she joined him, cupping her hands together. He put his left foot into her hands and swung his right leg up and across the horse. His momentum was greater than necessary and he would have gone right over the saddle if Jane hadn't grasped his belt and held him. He sighed with relief when his feet slid into the stirrups. But his head was aching intolerably and he closed his eyes.

Jane fetched her mount. She knotted Cole's reins together and wrapped them around her saddle horn.

'Don't give me any trouble,' she warned.

'I'm in no position to do that,' he replied irritably. 'Why don't you stop this nonsense right now? If you don't, I'll throw the book at you when I do get free.'

'What makes you think you'll come out of this alive?' she demanded.

Cole studied her face under the lantern-light and saw

that she was deadly serious. The knowledge pulled him up short, and coldness sneaked into his breast.

'You are serious!' he exclaimed. 'You would kill me if Floyd wanted that.'

'You'd better believe it,' she replied. 'Now let's hit the trail.'

She gigged her mount and led his horse out of the barn. Cole looked around desperately, hoping to see someone he knew who would intervene on his behalf, but the street was deserted; even Brady's saloon had closed its doors for the night. Jane set a fast pace out of town, and Cole gritted his teeth when the jolting of the pace jarred his skull into fresh and more powerful miseries.

The trail north was well illuminated by starlight, and a half-moon rode the clear sky above the eastern horizon. Cole worked on the knotted rope around his wrists but to no avail. He could not loosen its grip. He gave up eventually, hoping he would get a chance, however slim, to gain the upper hand in this situation. Jane pushed on with hardly a glance at him, and Cole realized that he would have to do something before they reached the Martin place. He did not relish the thought of falling into Floyd's hands if the ex-convict was in a revengeful mood, although he had done nothing to warrant this kind of treatment.

Dawn was greying the sky to the east, and as his range of vision increased, Cole picked out landmarks and knew exactly where they were. A mile separated them from the old Martin homestead that had lain derelict for more than ten years. Desperation began to loom larger in Cole's mind and he attacked his bonds once more, without success. They came within sight of a tumbledown shack

101

and a dilapidated barn as full daylight hit the range and the sun showed its face over on the eastern horizon.

A black horse was standing hipshot at a rail in front of the shack, its nose low to the ground. A movement in the doorway of the little building attracted Cole's gaze and he recognized the figure that emerged. Floyd Kennedy! His eyes glinted as he took in Floyd's appearance. The ex-convict did not look much different from the young man who had gone to prison. Breaking rocks for three years had kept him lean, but his face had some lines which had not been there before his incarceration. Floyd came out to where Jane had reined in and glowered at Cole.

'What the hell is he doing here?' he demanded.

'Is something wrong with your eyes?' Jane demanded. 'You said you wanted Paston so I brought the one I could get.'

'He's the wrong one. I don't want to kill him while he's riding for the law.' He glared at Cole. 'Where's Mart?'

'How the hell should I know? I'm not his keeper. He runs the Lazy P, so I guess that's where he'll be.'

'Well, he ain't there. I passed the ranch late yesterday afternoon, looking for him, and it was deserted. When I got to Squaw Creek I looked around for him, with the same result. So where is he?'

'Who shot up the law office last evening?' Cole demanded.

Floyd grinned. 'I was just letting Horden know I was back.'

'You shot him, and the doc doesn't know yet if he will live. It looks like you'll be straight back behind bars before you've had a chance to get used to being free, and with a charge of murder facing you.'

'Who's gonna arrest me?' Floyd's grin faded and his expression changed. 'I laughed when they told me in prison that you'd become a deputy. Ain't that a joke? So now you're a big man on account of that star, huh? Well, I'll soon cut you down to size, starting right now.'

'Untie my hands, give me a gun, and we'll settle this,' Cole rasped. 'I aim to arrest you for shooting the sheriff.'

'Talk's cheap.' Floyd took two swift paces forward and reached up to grasp Cole's shirt front. He hauled Cole out of the saddle and struck him with a right-hand blow. 'You ain't gonna do nothing, except die,' he grated.

Cole was dazed. His head was aching from the treatment he had received from Jane Kennedy. When Floyd's fist hit him his legs refused to hold him and he sprawled heavily on the ground, shaking his head. He heard Jane cry out, and looked up to see the girl dismounting swiftly. Floyd was drawing his pistol, and Jane flung herself at him, grasping his gun arm and thrusting his pistol aside as he aimed at Cole.

'Damn you, Jane, what in hell do you think you're doing?' Floyd said angrily.

'You're not going to shoot him in cold blood, Floyd,' she replied. 'I only agreed to help you because you said you wouldn't shoot anyone.'

'So I lied.' Floyd grinned. 'Get off my arm and let me finish him off.'

When Jane did not release him, Floyd lifted his left hand and slammed his hard knuckles into his sister's face. She uttered a cry and fell to the ground.

'You better do like I tell you,' Floyd rasped. 'There's trouble to be handled, and you've got to play your part.'

Floyd turned on Cole, who was getting shakily to his

feet. He swung his pistol and slammed the barrel towards Cole's face. Cole saw the blow coming and twisted sharply, lifting his left shoulder. The pistol struck his shoulder and he staggered back a pace, maintaining his balance with difficulty. Floyd cursed and surged forward, lifting his gun for another blow. Cole transferred his weight to his left foot and aimed a kick at Floyd's groin. Floyd ran on to the foot, yelled in agony, and fell away, his gun dropping from his grasp.

Cole tottered a few steps. He saw Floyd's gun lying in the dust but his hands were tied behind his back and he could not take advantage of the situation. He stepped in close to Floyd and kicked the ex-convict in the head, relishing the heavy contact made by his boot. Floyd relaxed instantly. Cole turned to where Jane was beginning to sit up. There was a streak of blood on her left cheek.

'Untie me, Jane,' Cole said urgently. 'Hurry, before he gets up and kills us. He's bent on his own trail and nothing will stop him.'

'He won't kill me,' she replied harshly, 'and he won't hit me again, ever.' She scrambled up and went to Cole's side. He turned his back to her and she tugged at the knots in the rope binding him. Cole felt a surge of relief as he was freed.

'Get your horse and pull out before Floyd gets up,' Jane said. 'I won't help him in whatever he's got planned.'

Cole bent and picked up Floyd's discarded gun. 'I can't leave,' he said. 'I'm gonna have to take Floyd in. If the sheriff dies then Floyd will be charged with murder.'

'Just leave,' she said forcefully. 'I'll take Floyd to the ranch and have Pa handle him.'

'You don't know that your pa has been out on the

warpath since yesterday.' Cole heaved a sigh and gave the girl details of the action that had taken place.

Jane shook her head, not wanting to believe what she was hearing.

'Pa said there'd be no trouble when Floyd got home,' she protested. 'What is going on that I don't know about?'

'There's a lot going on that most of us don't know about,' Cole replied. 'If you've got any sense, you won't want to get mixed up this. Ride back to town and stay there. I'll forget what happened between us, so you'll be clear as far as the law is concerned.'

'I'll ride out to the ranch and talk to my pa,' she responded.

'OK. But I'm gonna take Floyd in. He'll be safer behind bars until I can get some idea of what is going on.'

Jane did not object. She turned to her horse, swung into the saddle, and rode off without a backward glance. Cole heaved a sigh. His left arm, which had received a bullet slash the day before, was hurting. He had fallen on it when Jane hit him, and the wound had bled again. His left shoulder was sore where Floyd had caught him with the pistol, and the blow he had taken on the head had restarted the headache Jane had given him. He picked up the rope Jane had used on him and bound Floyd's hands behind his back before the ex-convict could regain his senses.

When Floyd's eyes flickered open Cole stirred him with the toe of his boot.

'On your feet, Floyd,' Cole said. 'You're going back behind bars.'

Floyd cursed him furiously.

'Stow that,' Cole said sharply. 'Keep your mouth shut.

All I want from you is word of what's going on. Why did you attempt to kill my brother Mart three years ago?'

'Go to hell!' Floyd gasped.

'You'll wind upon there before I do. Why did Mart shoot Frank Bartram before you tried to kill Mart? Did Bartram pay you to shoot Mart?'

'Ask your brother. It had nothing to do with me.'

'Bartram was shot dead in the doorway of the hotel yesterday. Did you kill him?'

'Why the hell would I wanta shoot Bartram?'

'I don't know. You tell me.'

'That's none of my business.'

Cole shook his head. 'OK, so get on your horse and we'll head back to town. You must like living behind bars.'

Floyd got to his feet and Cole thrust him up into his saddle. He swung into his own hull and took up Floyd's reins. The sun was peering above the horizon as they set out for the distant town.

Buster Askew reached Big G before sunup. He searched around for Mart Paston's body as the sun showed, and when he failed to find it he moved in closer to the Gifford ranch. The spread was just coming awake. Buster moved around the house in cover and studied the corral beside the barn. He looked over the dozen horses in the corral and grinned when he spotted Mart Paston's horse among them. He eased back and circled the yard until he could cover the entrance, and then settled down to wait.

In the ranch house Mart awoke on the couch where he had spent a restless night, and tried to assess the damage caused by Buck Kennedy's bullet. Pain stabbed through his left hip when he got up from the couch but he persevered and gained his feet. At that moment Hank Gifford came in to the big room.

'Hey, Mart, what are you doing?' Gifford demanded. 'Doc said you were to remain on your back until he returned. He should be back later today.'

'I'm worried about Cole,' Mart replied. 'I'm gonna ride to Lazy P and check it out before I go on to town. Kennedy tried to kill me yesterday, and I reckon he's gone to Squaw Creek to make a play for Cole.'

'But Cole was supposed to be heading out here with a posse,' Gifford protested.

'He should have been here by now. I don't like it. I think Kennedy has had a go at him, and I can't lie around here if Cole needs help. I think I'll be OK. I'll take it easy.'

Gifford could see that Mart would not be dissuaded from his intention. 'I'll have one of the boys saddle up your horse,' he said. 'Would you like someone to ride along with you?'

'Thanks, but I'd rather travel alone. It's open season on me right now, and I'd hate to drag any of your crew into my trouble.'

'Hell, you and Cole did a lot for Lance yesterday. He'd probably be dead now if you hadn't taken care of him. You better have breakfast before you pull out. Come and sit at the table, and I'll get cookie to pile a plate for you.'

Mart ate breakfast, and when he arose from the table afterwards the pain in his hip was intolerable. He took a few experimental steps, and was relieved when his discomfort lessened to a nagging ache. He went out to the porch. His horse was saddled and ready for travel. Hank Gifford was on the porch.

'I'll be surprised if you can stay in the saddle,' the

rancher said. 'But give it a try, if you have a mind to pull out.'

Mart approached his horse. His Winchester was snug in its saddle scabbard. He drew the long gun and checked it. Satisfied, he thrust the rifle back into its boot and stepped into his saddle from the porch. His hip protested until he put his feet into the stirrups, and then the pain eased back to a dull, nagging ache. He sat for a moment, checking out how he felt, and then lifted a hand to the watching Hank and touched spurs to his mount. By the time he reached the gate his hip was protesting more sharply, but he gritted his teeth and continued to ride.

He cleared the yard and headed towards the distant Lazy P, letting the horse travel at a pace that was between a trot and a canter. He looked around alertly, fearing an ambush from every likely spot he came across. The trouble on the day before had made him over-cautious. He had travelled a couple of miles when he began to suspect that he was being followed. It was nothing more than an itch between his shoulder blades, but he did not ignore it. He headed for a ridge, crossed it, and dropped down the other side until he was out of sight of his back trail.

Mart swung his mount around, drew his rifle, jacked a brass shell into the breech and gigged the horse back up towards the crest, reining in when he was just able to peer back along the trail. He pushed his hat back off his head and it hung down his back, suspended by its chin strap. The trail was empty. He could see a faint dust haze in the air, which marked his passing. He waited, fighting down his impatience. Three minutes later a rider appeared and came at a lope towards the spot where he was waiting.

Buster Askew! Mart recognized the BK gunman immediately. The last time he had seen Buster, the gunnie was a prisoner and being taken to jail by Cole. So what had happened?

Mart reined about and rode down the slope a couple of yards. He sat waiting for Buster to arrive, and minutes later the telltale beat of hoofs alerted him to Buster's imminent arrival.

Askew came over the crest as if he were on home range. When he saw Mart sitting his mount motionless and with levelled rifle, he uttered a curse of surprise and jerked on his reins to pull his horse around.

'Hold it,' Mart called. 'I've got one up the spout which has got your name on it.'

Askew had reached for his pistol instinctively, and it came smoothly into his right hand. Mart held his fire, hoping that Askew would realize that he was beaten, but the gunnie jerked his gun up into the aim. Mart triggered the long gun. Askew jerked back in his saddle as the crash of the shot smashed through the brooding silence of the morning. Mart reloaded quickly. He saw blood spurt from Askew's chest. Askew uttered a cry of pain, but still tried to bring his pistol into the aim. The Colt .45 rapidly grew too heavy for his hand and pulled free of his grip. Askew followed it out of his saddle and hit the ground.

Mart sat motionless until the echoes of the shot had faded away. He did not take his eyes off Askew's motionless figure. When full silence came he made the effort to dismount, and staggered across to where the gunnie was lying. He covered the still figure with his deadly rifle, and was surprised to see that Askew's eyes were open.

'Why didn't you throw down your gun?' Mart demanded.

Askew attempted to grin but could only manage a

grimace of pain. Blood dribbled from a corner of his mouth. He heaved a sigh and shrugged a shoulder. The bloodstain spreading through his shirt was right in the centre of his chest. He mumbled something which made no sense to Mart. Then he shuddered, stiffened, and relaxed in death. His eyes glazed over.

Mart turned to go back to his horse but heard the sound of approaching hoofs. He lifted his rifle, and the next instant a rider came over the crest and reined in quickly. Mart covered the newcomer until he recognized Hank Gifford.

'I was trailing you in case of trouble, and heard the shot,' Gifford said. 'Who's that?'

'Buster Askew.'

'I wish someone would tell me what is going on,' Gifford said.

'I think it's about time I told Cole what is going on,' Mart said tensely. 'I'd better head for town and talk to him. He's the one wearing the law badge. He ought to know what is happening, and why.'

'Is there anything I can do to help?' Gifford asked.

'No, Hank. I guess it is up to me. This has been going on for a long time, but I've kept quiet in the hope that it would all go away. Now I can see I was wrong, and I'll put matters right as soon as I get to town. If you see Cole before I do, tell him I'm looking for him, and I'll be waiting in town for him to show up.'

'OK.' Gifford sat his horse and watched Mart ride off towards town. Then he shook his head, swung his horse around, and rode on back to Big G, wondering at the mystery.

*

Jane Kennedy was thoughtful as she headed towards the BK. It was getting daylight, and she felt in two minds about returning home. She had stood by Floyd because he was family despite the bad mistakes he had made in his life, but she drew the line at cold-blooded murder, and when she saw that Floyd intended to kill Cole Paston she realized she could no longer support her brother. She did not know the rights or the wrongs of the trouble that had caused Floyd to be sent to prison, but she would not condone murder, for she was certain that Cole had done nothing to deserve such a fate. She headed homeward, determined to tell her father what had happened, and to seek his help in curbing Floyd.

The sun was above the horizon when she reached home range. She rode into the silent ranch and dismounted in front of the porch. A figure moved out of the shadows beyond a corner of the house, startling her.

'Who's there?' she called.

'Dave Walker. I'm watching the place because we got word trouble was coming. We're waiting for the boss to get back. We ain't seen hide or hair of him since yesterday morning, and before he rode out he talked of trouble coming.'

'I heard in town yesterday afternoon that he'd ridden in to talk to the sheriff,' Jane said. 'Don't worry about him, Dave. He's big enough to take care of himself.'

'He rode out with Mason and some of the gun hands, Jane, and it didn't look like a picnic they were going on. They were chasing big trouble, or I can't read sign. Say, have you seen anything of Floyd? They reckoned he would show up around here yesterday.'

'He's back,' she replied. 'I saw him in town. There was

trouble in Squaw Creek yesterday. Hank Bartram was shot dead outside his hotel, and the sheriff was gunned down.'

'You don't say!' Walker whistled through his teeth. 'I guessed there would be trouble when Floyd showed up again, but if he's responsible for Bartram and the sheriff then he's sure aiming high. I heard he had some unfinished business to settle when he got out of prison, but all the talk said his first target would be Mart Paston.'

'What went on three years ago between Floyd and Mart?' Jane demanded. 'The truth has never come out.'

'I never heard. There were rumours, but it had to be more than woman trouble. Mart Paston never seemed to bother about gals. He was wrapped up in Lazy P. And when Cole took to law dealing there wasn't room for anything else in his life. I don't know what the trouble was about, and I don't think anyone else does – except them who were involved.'

Jane sighed. 'Take care of my horse for me, Dave, will you?'

'Sure. Leave it to me. It'll give me something to do.' Walker reached out for the reins, and then swung around quickly and peered across the yard. 'Someone is coming,' he said.

Jane heard the sound of approaching hoofs and peered into the shadows. A rider materialized from a fold in the ground, slumped in his saddle, and came at a walk towards the porch.

'It's Pa!' she cried, recognizing the white stallion. 'And it looks like he's been hurt!'

Walker ran out, grasped the reins of the big white horse, and led the animal to the house. Buck Kennedy swayed in his saddle when the horse was halted, and then pitched sideways to the ground. Jane ran to his side.

'Pa, are you hurt bad?' she demanded, bending over him 'What happened to you?'

Kennedy was barely conscious. He was groaning. Jane could see a dark patch on the left shoulder of his pale shirt and pressed a hand against it.

'He's been shot,' she gasped. 'The blood has dried.'

'Let's get him into the house so we can look him over.' Walker tethered the stallion to the porch rail and went to open the door of the house. Jane peered at her father, her heart racing with fear.

'You take his legs,' said Walker. 'Let's get him inside.'

They lifted Kennedy with difficulty and carried him into the house, depositing his limp figure on a long couch. Walker unbuttoned the rancher's shirt to reveal a bullet wound just under the collarbone of the left shoulder.

'It doesn't look too bad,' Walker judged. 'If I had to take a slug then that's just about the spot I'd pick to have it.'

Jane looked at her father's pale, shock-filled features. 'I don't think Pa would agree with you,' she said. 'Get some water and some cloths, Dave. Then perhaps you'll ride into town and fetch Doc Carmody. I'll do what I can.'

Walker nodded and went into the kitchen. When he returned Jane busied herself tending her father, although there not much she could do. By the time she had made Kennedy comfortable his eyelids were flickering and he began to stir. When he opened his eyes he looked up at Jane for some moments without apparently recognizing her. Jane laid a tender hand on his forehead.

'How are you feeling, Pa?' she demanded. 'What happened to you?'

113

The sound of her voice brought Kennedy out of his shock.

'Have you seen Floyd?' he demanded.

'I saw him in town last night. Keep still, Pa. How did you get shot?'

'That doesn't matter. Why didn't Floyd come home straight from prison? What was he doing in town? Did he tell you what his plans are? When is he coming home?'

'He didn't say.' Jane shrugged. 'The last I saw of him, Cole Poston had arrested him.'

'What the hell for? Did Floyd break the law already?'

'He was planning to kill Cole.' Jane explained the incident.

'The young fool!' Buck Kennedy started up, but fell back. 'I stuck my neck out for him yesterday, to save him some trouble, but he's put his foot in it again. Dave, call some of the boys together. Tell them we're riding into town to bust Floyd outa the jail.'

'OK, boss.' Walker turned and headed for the door.

'Hold it right there, Dave,' Jane said. 'Pa, you're in no fit state to ride out. You'll stay here until the doctor has looked at you.'

Kennedy pushed himself into a sitting position on the couch, and then slumped sideways, groaning in pain. He pressed a hand to his shoulder and closed his eyes.

'It's obvious you're not going anywhere, Pa,' Jane said. 'If you think you are then try to get on your feet and make it to your horse.'

Kennedy shook his head.

'What shall I do, boss?' Walker demanded. 'You want some of the boys to ride in without you? We could bust that jail easy enough.'

114

'Forget it,' Kennedy said. 'Go fetch the doctor, Dave, and while you're there find out about Floyd. When I'm patched up we'll do what has to be done.'

Walker hurried out to the porch. Jane gazed at her father, her brow furrowed.

'Tell me what you did in town yesterday, Pa,' she said at length.

'Put some matters to rights, that's what,' Kennedy replied. 'I guessed that when Floyd came back he would want to pick up where he was at when they jailed him, but I reckoned I could do a better job so I went out and did it.'

'Did you shoot Frank Bartram?'

'Quit asking questions,' Kennedy snarled irritably. 'Get me something to eat and then I'll sleep. I need to be rested when the doc arrives. There's more shooting to be done.'

EIGHT

Cole was relieved when he saw Squaw Creek in the distance. The sun was well above the horizon and heat was beginning to pack into the low areas of the range. He glanced at Floyd. The ex-convict was slumped in his saddle, his face expressionless. He did not look up when Cole called to him, and Cole wondered what was going on in that devious mind. Floyd had always been a trouble-maker. He had gambled and raised hell around the county since he was old enough to buckle a gun belt around his waist. But he had overstepped the mark when he tried to kill Mart, and, now that he was branded with a spell in jail on his record, he would find no peace with law men out to put him back behind bars on the slightest pretext.

'Have you seen your pa since you got back?' Cole asked as their mounts kicked dust up on the main street.

'The hell I have!' Floyd broke his expression and scowled. 'Why would I wanta see him?'

'You sound like you got no feelings for him,' Cole observed. 'Buck cares a lot about you. He was raising hell around town yesterday, trying to troubleshoot for you so

116

you'd have it easy when you got home. This is no way to repay him.'

Floyd did not reply. They halted outside the law office. Cole dismounted and dragged Floyd out of his saddle. Charlie Swain emerged from the office and paused on the sidewalk. He looked as if he had not slept during the preceding night, and his face was set in grim lines.

'I'm sure glad to see you, Cole,' Swain greeted. 'There was some trouble here last night. One of the prisoners tried to grab my gun when I went to check on them. I pistol-whipped him for his trouble, forgetting the gun is hair-triggered, and it went off. The guy is dead. The other prisoner found his tongue after that. He told me the dead man was named Burt Riley, and they were paid to beat up the sheriff. It sure is hell, huh? Now who would want to put the sheriff out of action?'

'Did he say who paid them to do it?' Cole asked.

Swain shook his head. 'No, and he clammed up tight after that. I didn't even get his name outa him.'

Cole sighed. 'I got the other guy's name last night. He's Al Lockton. Let's put Floyd behind bars. I'm holding him on suspicion of shooting up this office with Lockton and Riley.'

'There was more trouble in town,' Swain went on. 'Last night, the bank guard, Len Porter, shot it out with Buck Kennedy outside Doc's place. Kennedy was hit but rode out of town, leaving Porter stretched out dead. Doc's wife said Kennedy was visiting her to ask about the sheriff, and, just after he left, the shooting took place. The banker, Bob Liffen, came into the office later and told me he'd had a visit from Buck Kennedy, who threatened to shoot him. He said Kennedy had told him that he, Kennedy, had shot

Frank Bartram yesterday afternoon. He said he could think of no reason why Kennedy should threaten him, and when Kennedy left, Liffen sent Porter to follow and watch him. He was shocked that it turned into a shooting. I told Liffen to see you when you got back, and he said he'd come in today and make a statement.'

'My pa wouldn't threaten Liffen,' Floyd cut in. 'They were real close; like brothers. You better find out what is going on, Paston. Someone is playing a deep game, and it looks like my pa is being set up.'

'We know Buck was on the warpath yesterday,' Cole replied. 'But I'll get to the bottom of it. Come on, into the cells. I've got work to do.'

When Floyd had been locked in a cell Cole felt as if a heavy weight had been lifted from his shoulders. He was tired and hungry, but there was no time to think of his own comfort. The office door was thrust open and Bob Liffen entered. The banker was dressed in a light-blue town suit. He was freshly shaved and looked sleek and well fed. Cole sat down behind the desk, feeling dishevelled. His head was still aching from the blows he had sustained in the night. The bullet slash in his left forearm was aching – his sleeve was stiff with dried blood. He put his hands to his head as Liffen began talking.

'You've heard about Porter being shot?' Liffen demanded.

'I've just this minute got the news,' Cole replied. 'So you had a visit from Buck Kennedy last evening and he threatened to kill you, huh?'

'That's right.' Liffen sat down on the chair placed before the desk.

'Why was he going to shoot you?' Floyd leaned his

118

elbows on the desk, studied the banker's tense face for a moment, and then asked, 'And why didn't he shoot you? He was shooting at everyone else yesterday.'

Liffen gazed at him, evidently thinking over the question. Then he shook his head. 'Hell, I don't know what was in his mind. He must have been drinking heavily before he came to see me. It was fortunate my bank guard was with me or God knows what might have happened. Kennedy told me he had shot Frank Bartram earlier. I didn't ask him why because he seemed to be in an unreasonable state of mind. When Kennedy left I told Porter to follow him and check out his movements. I was shocked when I heard there had been a shooting and that Porter was dead. The sooner you pick up Kennedy the better.'

'I want to know why Kennedy threatened to kill you,' Cole repeated.

'I don't know why! He didn't make any sense.'

'A man needs a good reason to talk of killing someone.' Cole shook his head. 'What's going on, Mr Liffen? Have you had any business dealings with Kennedy that turned sour? Or did you do something that riled him?'

'There was nothing like that.' Liffen got to his feet. 'Look, I'll make a statement whenever you like but I won't keep you now. I expect you'll be busy over the next few days.'

Cole suppressed a sigh. 'OK, I'll be in touch with you later if I need you.' He watched as the banker hurriedly departed.

'What do you make of him?' asked Charlie Swain.

'Liffen knows more than he's telling, so what has he got to hide?' Cole shook his head. 'Charlie, I'm gonna have to eat, and then clean up. After that, I need to see how the

119

sheriff is doing. Doc should be back from Big G by now, and I need him to look at my arm. Can you hold on here for another hour?'

'I've got all day,' Swain replied. 'You go and do what's needed. You don't have to worry about this place. Pierce will show up shortly, and we'll handle the chores between us.'

Cole nodded and got to his feet. 'It's a bad thing the sheriff was shot,' he declared. 'He's had more experience in law dealing than me. I don't know what the hell to do next.'

'Visit him,' Swain suggested. 'He might be awake, and maybe he can tell you something about what's going on in town. He was always snooping around, and if anyone has any idea of what's happening, then he's the man.'

Cole nodded and went to the door. 'I'll check on him right now,' he decided.

He left the office and walked along the street to Doc Carmody's office. Mrs Carmody answered the door to his knock. She looked as if she hadn't slept during the night, and greeted him with a relieved smile.

'I'm so glad to see you, Cole,' she said. 'Come on in. What's wrong with your arm?'

'Is Doc back from the Gifford place?' Cole asked.

'He came home an hour ago, but was called out to the Sutton homestead before he could sit down. He saw your brother Mart out at Big G. There had been some shooting and Mart was wounded. Doc patched him up, and said his life was not in any danger.'

Col was shocked by the news. Impatience filled him but he curbed it. 'I hope Mart will come into town,' he said. 'How is the sheriff?'

120

'He seems to be making progress. Doc thinks he will make a full recovery. Pete was awake earlier, and spoke to Doc. Do you want to see him?'

'I need to ask him some questions,' Cole said.

He entered the house and followed Mrs Carmody up the stairs to a back bedroom. The sheriff was propped up on a couple of pillows. His eyes were closed, his face ashen in shock, and he looked to have aged ten years. He was stripped to the waist and heavy bandaging covered his left shoulder. He was breathing heavily. The room was hot despite the window being open. Cole felt stifled and drew a deep breath as the pain in his head seemed to worsen.

'I'll leave you,' said Mrs Carmody. 'Talk to him, and he might come to his senses if he hears a voice he knows.'

Cole approached the bed and sat down on a chair beside it. He leaned forward, his elbows on his knees.

'Hey, Pete, can you hear me?' he said in a low tone. 'I've got a lot of trouble at the moment, and I need to pick your brains. Open your eyes and talk to me.'

Horden did not stir. His breathing was ragged. He was sweating. Cole kept talking, trying to stir the wounded man back to his senses. At first it seemed that he would be unsuccessful, but after some minutes Horden muttered, then stirred uneasily. His eyes flickered open. He gazed up at Cole without recognition.

'How are you doing, Pete?' Cole asked.

Horden drew a deep breath and exhaled slowly. His eyes lost their uncertainty. 'Cole,' he said in a wavering voice. 'It's good to see you, son. What happened?'

Cole explained, and Horden moved restlessly. He nodded as his mind began to recall the events of the previous day.

121

'I remember most of it now,' he said. 'I took that badge off you yesterday, so why are you still wearing it?'

'When you were shot I had to pin it back on, Pete. Someone has got to run the department while you're out of it. Just listen to what I have to tell you. All hell broke loose and I don't know where to begin the clean-up.' He listed the incidents that had taken place. Horden listened intently; his eyes were unblinking. When Cole lapsed into silence the sheriff shook his head.

'I was afraid this would happen,' he said in a mumble, as if his lips could not keep pace with his thoughts. 'I could smell trouble coming, but there was nothing I could do to stop it. We kept quiet about our business all those years ago, but I was always afraid that it would come out like this.'

'You're talking in riddles,' Cole said. 'Ain't it about time you gave it to me straight? You seem to know what is going on but you're out of it for a spell, and I have to pick up the pieces. For God's sake open up so I can stop the trouble before someone else gets killed.'

'I don't think it can be stopped now,' Harden said.

'Tell me what you know, anyway,' Cole insisted.

'Give me a drink of water.' Horden motioned to a bedside table. 'I'm burning up. You shouldn't be bothering me at this time, Cole. I've done my duty around here for nigh on thirty years, and I ain't done a bad job. This is the first time I've been laid low, so give me a break and let me rest. I'll sort out the trouble when I get back on my feet.'

'That ain't good enough, Pete.' Cole poured water from a jug into a glass and lifted the sheriff's head before putting the glass to his lips. Horden drank greedily. 'Liffen told me Buck Kennedy admitted killing Frank Bartram, so shouldn't I pull Kennedy in? He's the one been causing all the trouble. He came to the Lazy P while I was there yesterday, and his foreman took a shot at Mart, which started off a whole shooting-match.'

'It won't end now it has started.' Horden shook his head. 'There are some bad men in the county hiding behind respectable faces, and they are afraid of being exposed.'

'And you're one of them,' Cole said sharply. 'That's got to be the answer, Pete. What was it you got mixed up in?'

'What the hell!' Horden tried to sit up but the effort was too much for him and he fell back on his pillow, a groan spilling from his lips. 'Who told you that, Cole?'

'You shouldn't drink too much if you've got secrets on your mind, Pete. I've heard you muttering about a robbery you pulled with an outlaw gang thirty years ago. I didn't hear you mention where the robbery took place, but you talked about Frank Bartram sometimes, so I figured he was one of the gang. What about it, Pete? Tell me what is going on.'

Horden closed his eyes. Cole watched him for some moments, and when it seemed that the sheriff was not going to answer his questions he grasped Horden's right arm.

'Hey, Pete, don't clam up on me,' he said. 'I need information, and I want it now. Come on, talk to me!'

Horden snored softly, his eyelids flickering. Cole was certain the sheriff was pretending to be asleep or unconscious, and he stifled a sigh.

'OK,' he said at length. 'If that's the way you wanta play it then I'll do some investigating on my own, and I'll arrest anyone I find was mixed up with a gang of outlaws. If it does come out that you were a bank robber then I'll come for you and stick you behind bars, Pete. You better think about it. I'll get back to you later, but don't expect any favours if I have to root this out for myself.'

He waited, but the sheriff did not twitch a muscle. Suppressing a sigh, Cole left the room, filled with a sudden determination, aware that the news about Mart getting shot had pushed him into a corner. He left the house and went back to the law office. Swain was seated at the desk, reading a newspaper. He looked up.

'Floyd wants to see Harmon, the lawyer, because he says he hasn't done anything wrong,' Swain reported. 'OK if I send for him?'

'Sure.' Cole grimaced. 'I'm holding Floyd for shooting the sheriff. If Harmon comes in, you can tell him why Floyd is behind bars and that I'll hold him until I can check him out. I'm going after Liffen now. I'm not satisfied with the way he's acting. I need to learn what he knows.'

He departed again and walked to the bank. When he entered he found Liffen standing just inside the main door, talking to Joseph Brant, the teller. Liffen's eyes narrowed at the sight of Cole.

'We need to talk some more, Mr Liffen,' Cole said.

'I told you all I know. I'm a very busy man, Cole. It will have to wait.'

'There are two ways of handling this,' Cole responded. 'You can talk to me now, or I can drag you along to the jail and leave you to sweat in a cell for a few hours before I get around to you.'

'What do you want?' Liffen hesitated, then said: 'Come

into my office.'

Cole followed the banker into the office and closed the door. Liffen went behind his desk and sat down. Cole sat on a chair beside the desk. He sighed wearily as he watched Liffen, who riffled nervously through a sheaf of papers on the pretext of being busy.

'Why did Buck Kennedy threaten to shoot you?' Cole asked.

'I told you I don't know, and I wasn't about to ask him. He'd already told me he shot Frank Bartram, and I believed him when he said he would shoot me.'

'What do you know about a bank robbery that happened about thirty years ago?' Cole, watching Liffen intently, saw a change of mood seep into the man's expression. Liffen's eyes widened and for a few seconds fear shone in their depths. 'That hit a nerve, huh?' Cole continued. 'I think you'd better to come clean and tell me what you know.'

'Who told you about a bank robbery?' Liffen demanded. His face had paled and his nervousness grew. He interlaced his fingers to stop the trembling that assailed them.

'Sheriff Horden! He's wounded and badly shocked, but I believe him. He told me he rode with an outlaw gang thirty years back. Frank Bartram was mentioned, and there are one or two others who took part in the robbery. My guess is that Buck Kennedy was also one of the gang and, the way you're acting now, I suspect you are another who was involved.'

'That's a lie!' Liffen leaned forward in his seat and put his elbows on the desk. Beads of sweat suddenly appeared on his forehead and he cuffed them away. 'What did

Horden tell you exactly?' he demanded.

'It's not for me to answer your questions,' Cole rasped. 'It's up to you to come clean, and if I don't get a satisfactory answer then I'll stick you in a cell.'

'Kennedy killed Bartram, so why don't you rope him in and ask him why?'

'I'll get around to Kennedy later,' Cole promised.

'And when you catch up with him, ask him why he killed your father!'

'Killed my father?' Cole felt a cold pang stab through the pit of his stomach. His father, Mike Paston, had died four years earlier when he had been thrown by his horse. 'What are you talking about, Liffen? Are you trying to side-track me?'

'Mike Paston's death was made to look like an accident, but he was murdered to shut his mouth. He had begun talking about the old days; naming men he had ridden with, and that was why he was murdered. Ask Buck Kennedy about it. He's the one should be in jail. You're wasting your time talking to me.'

Cole was shocked by the allegation, and his brain whirled. He would never forget the terrible day when word was brought out to Lazy P that his father was dead; killed by his horse, and he had never understood how a man of his father's experience could have been thrown and stomped.

'If you know my father was murdered then you must be aware of who did it, Liffen, and why.' Cole spoke through clenched teeth. 'I'm giving you a chance to tell me what I need to know but my patience is wearing thin. If you know anything at all then open up. If you don't I'll take you out of here at gunpoint and jail you.'

126

Liffen gazed at Cole with panic flaring in his mind. He had already said too much, but he had needed to turn Cole's attention from himself. He'd had no intention of mentioning Mike Paston, but it was out in the open now and he could not retract the statement. He could see that Cole was wound up tight, and he began to fear the consequences.

'Buck Kennedy told me he'd killed your father.' Liffen moistened his lips.

'Will you make a statement to that effect?' Cole demanded.

'Sure, if you promise that you won't involve me in anything until after Kennedy is behind bars. He'd kill me for sure if he heard that I'd spilled the beans.'

'I won't let Kennedy get within a mile of you once I've arrested him. Write out your statement about my father's death. Do it now. Use a sheet of your bank notepaper. I'll hang fire on the rest of this trouble until I've got Buck Kennedy in custody.'

Liffen nodded and began to write his statement. Cole watched with his mind in turmoil.

'Why did Kennedy kill my father? How would my pa know about that bank robbery?'

'Can't you guess?' Liffen looked up at Cole. His lips were twisted into a caricature of a smile but doubt showed in his expression. 'Mike was one of the gang that pulled the robbery – at the bank in Mulejaw Bend, west of here. A teller was killed in the raid. It was in the local paper at that time.'

'And how do you know so much about it? You must have been one of the robbers. Is that why Buck Kennedy threatened to kill you?'

127

Liffen shook his head. 'I can't answer that,' he responded.

'Because your answer would incriminate you, I guess.' Cole nodded. 'OK, get on with the statement, and don't leave anything out.'

Liffen wrote hesitatingly, as if he found it difficult to recall what had occurred all those years ago, unless, Cole thought bleakly, he was trying to frame his statement to avoid being implicated in the bank raid. When Liffen had finished, be signed his name, then handed the statement to Cole.

'That's how I remember it,' Liffen said. 'It happened thirty years ago, but I can recall every detail of it.'

Cole read the statement, which named Buck Kennedy, Frank Bartram and Mike Paston as participants in the robbery.

'How do you know so much about it, Liffen, if you weren't there?' Cole demanded.

'That's all I've got to say about it.' Liffen grimaced. 'That's more than enough to go on. You'd better pick up Buck Kennedy now. He's running wild, and he won't stop now until he's killed everyone who is connected to that bank raid.'

'I guess you won't be going anywhere,' Cole mused, 'so I'll know where to find you if I need you again.'

He folded the statement, tucked it into the breast pocket of his shirt, and then went to the door to leave. He heard the sound of a drawer being jerked open and swung round quickly to see Liffen lifting a gun from his desk. The banker's face was contorted into an expression of desperation. Cole reached instinctively for the gun in his holster, and Liffen cocked his pistol, his lips pulling back from his teeth in a snarl.

'I don't want to have to shoot you in here,' Liffen said through clenched teeth, 'but I will do so without hesitation, if you force me to. Get you hands up and turn your back to me. I'll take your gun, and then we'll slip out the back door and go to my house. You know too much, Cole.'

'You won't get away with it,' Cole said.

'I have no option but to try. You're the only one who knows the identity of the Mulejaw bank robbers, and with you out of the way I can carry on here as if nothing had happened. You've pushed your nose into my business, Cole, and this is the only way out.'

Cole studied Liffen's face. He could tell that the banker was deadly serious, and a shiver of tension filtered through him as he lifted his hands shoulder high and turned his back. Liffen's chair scraped and the next moment Cole felt his pistol being snatched from his holster. He did not need to be told that he was in dire trouble.

NINE

Mart Paston had to summon up all of his determination to stay in the saddle until he reached Squaw Creek. The dull ache in his left hip became an almost intolerable agony as the miles passed, and when he eventually sighted the little cow town he was keen to quit his torturous saddle, but he clenched his teeth, continued into the main street, and rode to the law office. He wanted more than anything to see his brother Cole. The position of the sun told him the time was nearing noon, and he heaved a long sigh of relief as he slid out of his saddle and felt solid ground beneath his feet. He clung to the saddle, closed his eyes, and waited hopefully for his weakness to recede.

He heard the door of the law office open; boots sounded on the sidewalk, and then a hand touched his shoulder.

'Hey, Mart, are you OK?' Charlie Swain demanded. 'Anything I can do to help?'

'Is Cole around?' Mark lifted his head. 'I need to see him real bad.'

'He ain't here right now,' Swain replied. 'He went to see Liffen at the bank. You better come into the office and sit down before you fall down. Come on, I'll give you a hand.'

Mart closed his eyes as Swain helped him, and kept them closed until he was seated in the chair behind the desk. Then he looked up at Swain.

'You look like you need the doc to check you out, Mart.' Swain's face expressed concern. 'You look like death, pard, and you're covered in blood. Sit here and rest. I'll go hunt up Cole. Will you be all right while I'm gone?'

'I'm not dead yet,' Mart replied. 'I thought Cole would have taken a posse out to BK by now to pick up Buck Kennedy. Why is he wasting time with the likes of Bob Liffen?'

'There's been a lot of trouble around here these past twenty-four hours,' Swain said. 'You wouldn't believe the half of it. Last night, Buck Kennedy killed Len Porter, Liffen's bank guard. They shot it out in front of Doc Carmody's office. Liffen came in to talk about Porter being killed, and he told Cole Buck Kennedy had threatened to kill him. He said Kennedy admitted killing Frank Bartram.'

'Jeez!' Mart drew a deep breath. 'I killed Buster Askew this morning. He was laying for me this side of Big G.'

'Cole has been busy too. He rode in earlier with Floyd Kennedy under arrest, and said Floyd shot up this office with the help of two hardcases. It was in that shoot-out that the sheriff was wounded.'

'You've got Floyd here, behind bars?' Mart demanded.

'He sure looked like he was locked up back there the last time I looked in at him,' Swain retorted.

'I want to talk to him, Charlie.'

'I don't see what good that would do,' Swain objected. 'Wait until Cole comes back. He should be along any time now.'

'I can't wait.' Mart pushed himself erect and staggered out from behind the desk. 'We've got to grab Buck Kennedy and stick him in a cell with Floyd. Buck went over the top yesterday, and there's no telling what he'll do next.'

'Len Porter put a bullet in him last night, so he won't be feeling too spry today. Say, you look ready to drop, so sit down and rest while I fetch Cole.'

'You'd be surprised what a man can push himself to do when he's desperate,' Mart said, shaking his head. 'I'll look for Cole.'

He walked unsteadily to the door and departed, but when he reached the sidewalk he paused and pressed a hand to his left hip. Pain was throbbing through his wound and he waited for it to subside. He peered around the street, and for some odd reason it did not look familiar to him. The sun was glaring down, hurting his eyes. He drew a deep breath and held it for a moment, summoning up what was left of his strength and willpower.

When his spasm of weakness passed, Mart limped towards the bank, impatient to catch up with Cole. The bank was deserted when he entered. Joseph Brant, the teller, a tall, thin, middle-aged man, had a long face that was lean and angular, brown eyes perpetually narrowed. His lank hair was black. He looked unkempt despite wearing a blue town suit. Brant was behind a grille, busy with book-work, and he did not look up immediately when Mart's figure fell across him. His lips were moving soundlessly as he totted up a column of figures.

'Be with you in a moment,' he said, not pausing in his sums. He reached the bottom of a column, made a note beneath it, and then looked up. 'Howdy, Mart?' he greeted. 'You look like you've been in a war. How can I help you?'

'I'm looking for Cole,' Mart replied. 'I was told he came in to see Mr Liffen.'

'That's right.' Brant nodded. 'He came in earlier, as I remember. But I didn't see him leave – I had a rush of customers about then. Cole went into the office with Mr Liffen, but when I went to speak to Mr Liffen shortly after, Cole was gone, and so had Mr Liffen.'

'Did they leave together?'

Brant shook his head. 'I didn't see either of them leave. But then they might have gone out the back door. I'm surprised Mr Liffen didn't tell me he was leaving. Is there some kind of trouble, do you know? It isn't like Mr Liffen to quit the bank at any time while it is open for business.'

'There's been trouble around town over the past twenty-four hours,' Mart said, 'and out on the range too, for that matter. Do you know where Liffen might have gone?'

'Home, probably.' Brant shrugged. 'Although I can't imagine why he would take Cole there.'

Mart turned away and departed. He entered the alley that led to the square of private houses owned by the prominent members of the community, and as he reached the corner of Liffen's house he saw the banker emerging from the front door. Liffen paused to lock the door, turned to leave, and was confronted by Mart. Liffen started violently, his expression changing instantly. Mart saw undisguised fear revealed in the banker's narrowed eyes. Liffen looked around quickly, as if searching for a way of escape, and took a half-step to his left. Mart shot out a hand and grasped the banker's arm.

133

'Hold up there,' he said sharply. 'I want to talk to you, Mr Liffen.'

'What do you want with me?' Liffen gasped.

'Cole saw you in the bank earlier, and he hasn't been seen since. Where is he?'

'I don't know. He left me after a few minutes. Do you think I have the time to watch his movements?'

'What did he see you about?' Mart persisted. He regarded Liffen with suspicion because the banker seemed so nervous. Liffen was plainly ill at ease, and sweat beaded his forehead.

'Len Porter, my bank guard, was shot dead last night by Buck Kennedy – murdered, in fact,' Liffen said in a nervous rush. 'Cole wanted to know what Kennedy had to say to me when he visited me last night. Kennedy threatened to kill me, and he told me he'd killed Bartram yesterday afternoon. I don't know what the world is coming to. The violence in this country is getting worse instead of better, and we are supposed to be civilized! You'll have to excuse me now; I have to get back to the bank.'

Mart stood and watched Liffen hurry away, frowning as he considered the banker's manner. He wondered what Liffen had to feel guilty about, for the man had seemed like a youth caught red-handed in some sinful act. And where was Cole? If he had left the bank after finishing his business he would surely have returned to the law office. Mart turned away and went back to the main street. He searched for Cole, checking the bars, the restaurant and the hotel, but no one seemed to have seen his brother. He even went along to the livery barn to check if Cole had ridden out, but his horse was in a stall. He returned to the

134

law office to find Charlie Swain seated at the desk.

'Where's Cole?' Swain demanded.

'Hasn't he come back?' Mart demanded.

'Hell! I ain't seen hide or hair of him.'

'And I've been along the street asking after him, but nobody has seen him.'

'He was talking about getting some food and then changing his clothes,' Swain said.

'I've checked the eating house – they haven't seen him.' Mart explained about Liffen; how the man had reacted when confronted, and Swain grimaced.

'That doesn't sound too good, Mart,' he mused. 'You should have seen Liffen in here last night when Cole began to question him. If ever a man looked guilty about something then Liffen did. He almost ran out of the office when Cole pressed him about a bank robbery that took place in Mulejaw Bend about thirty years ago.'

'What did Cole say about that bank job?' Mart demanded.

'You sound like you know something about it. What gives, Mart?'

'I heard about it,' Mart said heavily,' but I didn't think Cole knew of it. I wonder how he heard. I need to talk to Floyd, Charlie. Perhaps he said something to Cole.'

'What the hell has Floyd got to do with it? He ain't been around in a coon's age.'

'He's known about that robbery a long time. It was the reason he went to jail for trying to kill me. I'd heard he'd said my father was in the gang that robbed the Mulejaw bank, and when I faced him about it he pulled his gun on me.'

Swain gazed at Mart, his face expressing disbelief, then

he picked up the keys and led the way into the cell block at the rear of the office. Mart saw Floyd Kennedy sitting on a bunk in a cell and went to the door. He gazed silently at Floyd for some moments, and Floyd stared sullenly back at him.

'Have you come to gloat?' Floyd demanded. 'You won't be so happy when I get out of here and come for you with a gun.'

'You tried that once before,' Mart replied. 'What makes you think you'll have better luck next time?'

'I'll kill you the minute I get the chance,' Floyd rasped.

'You seemed to know a lot about the Mulejaw bank robbery before you went to jail,' Mart said. 'So who was in on that job?'

'Your pa was.' Floyd grinned. 'You don't like that, huh?'

'And who else? Cole reckoned the sheriff let it out that he ran with a gang when he was a young man. Was the sheriff one of the robbers?'

'That's none of my business,' Floyd responded harshly.

'You were keen to tell me three years ago about my pa being involved. Why, Floyd?'

'Because you were interested in Polly Ellard and I told her about your pa to put her off you. I fancied Polly, but even when she knew the truth she didn't wanta know me, so I reckoned to put you away permanent.'

'How did you know about my pa, Floyd? Who told you he was in that gang?'

'I don't remember.' Floyd shook his head. 'It ain't important. Let me out of here, stick a gun in my hand, and we'll see who walks away afterwards.'

'Let's go find Cole,' Charlie Swain cut in. 'You're wasting time here, Mart, and Cole could be in real trouble

136

right now. What's all this talk about something that happened thirty years ago?'

'Sure.' Mart turned away. 'Floyd ain't leaving. He'll be here when I get back.'

'And I ain't gonna talk to you,' Floyd called as Mart returned to the office.

'I wish I knew what that was all about.' Swain locked the door between the office and the cells. 'Listen, Mart, It looks like Cole found trouble this morning when he went to the bank. The way Liffen was acting last night, you'd have thought he was caught up in that bank robbery at Mulejaw Bend. He's the last man to see Cole this morning, and you caught him coming out of his house when everyone knows he never leaves the bank while it is open for business.'

'So?' Mart demanded.

'So I reckon we should go take a look in Liffen's house to see if Cole is there.'

Mart was puzzled. 'Why would Cole be in Liffen's house?' he demanded.

'Maybe Liffen tied him up, or something.' Swain's face was deadly serious.

'Are you joshing me, Charlie?'

'The hell I am. I saw the way Liffen acted last night. He was shaking in his shoes. I wondered then why he was so het up. He sure looked guilty as hell about something. Are you coming with me or do I go alone? I know Cole would have come back to the office if he was able to, so this has got to be checked out.'

Mart gazed at Swain while his mind tried to accept what had been said. 'I think you're crazy,' he said at length. 'We can't just go and break into Liffen's house.'

'That much I know.' Swain nodded. 'I reckon it would be easier to get Liffen to take us there.'

'He wouldn't do that in a hundred years!'

'He would, with a little persuasion.' Swain tapped the butt of his holstered Colt. 'What have we got to lose? If Liffen refuses then it would point to his guilt, as far as I'm concerned.'

Mart drew his pistol, and checked it before sliding it back into his holster. His face was harshly set as he went to the door. 'What are you waiting for, Charlie?' he demanded.

They went to the bank. The teller was busy with a customer. There was no sign of Liffen. Swain nudged Mart in the direction of the banker's office.

'You'd better leave the talking to me, Mart,' Swain said. 'I am a special deputy, and I can take over when the sheriff and Cole aren't around.'

Mart grimaced and drew a deep breath. Swain opened the door to Liffen's office and entered quickly. He saw Liffen seated behind his desk and dropped his right hand to the butt of his holstered gun. Liffen looked up as Mart entered and closed the door. His expression changed instantly. He half-arose from his seat, then dropped back into it, his shock changing to fear.

'What do you want?' Liffen blustered. 'You've got no right to come busting in here.'

'Cole Paston ain't been seen around town since he came in here to talk to you earlier,' Swain said officiously. 'So what have you done with him, Liffen?'

Liffen's face turned pale. 'How dare you come in here making such an accusation?' he demanded. 'Cole left here more than an hour ago.'

138

'No one saw him leave, and he ain't been seen around since,' Swain said doggedly.

'That's probably because he didn't want to be seen,' Liffen replied. 'He asked to leave by the back door and I showed him out. He seemed to have a lot on his mind, and I'm not surprised, considering all the trouble we've had around here these last two days.'

'Did he say where he was going?' Mart cut in.

'He didn't, and I wouldn't expect him to tell me his business. Now you'd better get out of here before I lodge a complaint about your behaviour.'

'You ain't cutting any ice with me by using that tone,' Swain said sharply. 'Get up and take us to your house. We're making a search of the town for Cole, and your place is next on the list.'

'You're loco!' Liffen pulled open a drawer in his desk and reached inside.

Mart shouted a warning and made a grab for his pistol. He saw Liffen's hand appear, clutching a gun, and knew he was too slow to prevent the banker from firing the weapon. But Swain was not taken by surprise. He palmed his gun the instant Liffen's hand closed upon the pistol, and he was covering the banker before Liffen could fire.

'Drop it,' Swain said coldly. 'I reckon you're in enough trouble as it is without adding to it. We're gonna look in your house, with or without your permission, Mr Liffen, and we'll do it now.'

Liffen dropped his gun back into the drawer and got to his feet, his face set in a sullen scowl.

'We'll leave like Cole did,' said Swain. 'Out the back door and straight to your house. Come on, let's go.'

Liffen looked at the gun in Swain's hand, aware that

139

there was nothing he could do but obey. He got up from his chair and went to the back door. Swain followed the banker closely, his gun ready, and Mart tagged along behind. They crossed the back lots to the huddle of houses, and Liffen made no comment until he reached his front door.

'You're making a big mistake, Swain,' he said, 'and it'll cost you your job. I am a member of the town council, and you can't treat me like a common criminal.'

'Get on with it,' Swain said impatiently. 'Unlock the door.'

Liffen felt in several pockets before he produced the key to the door. Mart, watching the banker closely, could tell that he was playing for time. When Liffen failed to get the key into the lock, Mart snatched the key from him, pushed him aside, and unlocked the door. Swain thrust Liffen in over the doorstep. Liffen turned quickly, a cry of desperation gusting from his lips. He grabbed at Swain's gun hand, tried to push the muzzle aside, failed, and then caught hold of the barrel and jerked the gun towards himself in a desperate attempt to pull it out of Swain's gasp. The weapon exploded with a report that echoed across the town. Liffen was struck by the bullet, and the impact hurled him back a couple of steps. Blood spurted from his chest and he slumped to the floor.

Swain was shocked. 'Hell!' he gasped. 'This gun is hair-triggered. He shouldn't have grabbed it.'

'He looks like he's dead,' Mart said. 'Come on. Let's search the house before anyone shows up.'

'And if Cole ain't here?' Swain demanded, white-faced in shock.

'You should have thought of that before we braced

140

Liffen,' Mart responded.

Mart entered the house and began a search. Liffen lived alone. The ground-floor rooms were deserted. Mart ascended the stairs. He checked the main bedroom at the front of the house and found nothing. Swain trailed along behind him. Mart opened the door of a small back room and paused on the threshold. Cole was trussed and gagged on a bed. Mart went forward thankfully and untied Cole, who was conscious and apparently unhurt. Mart hastily freed Cole, who sprang to his feet.

'I heard a shot!' Cole gasped. 'What happened, Mart?'

Mart explained. Cole ran from the room before Mart could give him all the facts and Mart followed his brother down the stairs to find Cole examining Liffen. Cole straightened.

'He's dead,' he announced, 'and I badly needed to talk to him.'

'It was an accident,' Swain said ruefully. 'But you've got some explaining to do, Cole. Why were you hogtied in Liffen's house?'

'Because I got too close to the truth about what's been happening. I don't know how Liffen was involved in this trouble, but obviously he was in it up to his neck. Now he's dead, and we'll never know what happened. This is a real mess, and I only hope the sheriff will pull through. If I can get the truth out of him we might be able to clear this up.'

'Don't forget Buck Kennedy,' Mart said. 'Why did he go on the rampage yesterday if he wasn't involved? He killed Bartram, I heard, and threatened Liffen last night. I reckon Kennedy has got some of the answers, Cole.'

'And I'm heading out right now to pick him up,' Cole said hastily. 'Charlie, get a posse together and we'll ride to

BK. It's time we got down to some serious law dealing.'

'Now you're talking my language.' Swain grinned and departed hurriedly. He paused in the doorway and looked back at Cole. 'I'll have a dozen men ready to ride in thirty minutes,' he said.

'So what happened out at Big G, Mart?' Cole demanded.

Mart explained as they left the banker's house. Cole closed and locked the door, and then dropped the key into a pocket. He listened to Mart's account of the incidents that had taken place on the range.

'You said you recognized Buck Kennedy after he shot you?' he asked when Mart lapsed into silence.

'I didn't see him clearly. He was cursing his horse, like he always does, and I recognized his voice.'

'Then I'll get ready to ride out with the posse,' Cole said. 'Your evidence will do to hold Kennedy. You'd better stay in the office and rest up until I get back, Mart.'

'That suits me.' Mart heaved a long sigh of relief. 'Take Kennedy alive, Cole. He's got a lot of talking to do.'

'You bet!' Cole replied. 'I'll handle him with gloves on. When I get back, Mart, we've got some talking to do.'

'I'll be waiting for you,' Mart replied grimly.

TEN

Jane Kennedy spent the morning waiting for Doc Carmody to show up at the BK ranch, and by noon, with no sign of the doctor arriving, her patience became exhausted. Her father was sleeping restlessly on the couch in the big front room, and she had checked him regularly during the morning. But he did not awaken until she had decided to leave him and head for town to discover what had happened to Floyd. She changed her clothes, and was on her way to the front door when Buck Kennedy sat up and called to her.

'Where the hell are you going?' he demanded.

'I can't sit around any longer, Pa,' she replied. 'I'm worried about Floyd. You can't do anything about him so it is up to me. I'm going into town, and if I can get him out of jail I'll handle it.'

'No you won't!' Kennedy pushed his feet off the couch and sat up, stifling a groan of pain. He got to his feet, stood swaying for a moment, and then shrugged his shoulders. 'A good sleep was all I needed. I ain't gonna let a little thing like a slug in the shoulder keep me from doing what has to be done. I ain't feeling too bad right now. Get me some breakfast and then I'll ride out. I ain't settled the Giffords at Big G yet, and it's about time they got their come-uppance. But I guess I'd better ride into town and pull Floyd out of his trouble. You stay here, out of the way. I don't want you getting under my feet.'

Jane knew better than to argue with her father so she did not protest. She fetched him cold food from the kitchen and watched him devour it. When he was drinking coffee, he looked over the rim of the cup and spoke sharply.

'Tell the crew to saddle up. I want them to ride with me this morning. Get someone to saddle up my chestnut. I'll be leaving shortly.'

'You'd better not ride, Pa,' she protested. 'You'll open up your wound if you do. Pay heed to me, please.'

Kennedy did not answer. Jane suppressed a sigh and went out to the porch. She saw one of the crew working by the corral and crossed to him.

'Tell the crew to get ready to ride out with my pa, Hank,' she instructed, 'and saddle up the chestnut for my father. Bring it over to the porch. Pa's set on riding into town to cause more trouble, and I believe the local law will be out to put him behind bars.'

'He's righting some wrongs,' Hank observed, 'and we'll back him all the way.'

'He's been causing trouble, whatever the rights and wrongs are,' Jane insisted.

Hank shrugged and went over to the corral. Jane hurried back to her father. He was drinking whiskey from a bottle, and smacked his lips when he set it down.

'That's better,' he said. 'I'll be riding out now. Don't

144

forget what I told you. Stay here until I get back.'

'What are you going to do?' she demanded.

'You should know better than to ask. I'm clearing the trail for Floyd. I want his homecoming to be free of any trouble.'

Kennedy drew his pistol, checked its loads, and then thrust it back into its holster. He went out to the porch and stood leaning against a post until his horse was brought over from the corral. He stifled a groan as he stepped up into his saddle but ignored the pain and touched spurs to the chestnut. Jane emerged from the house to watch his departure, her eyes filled with foreboding. Six of the outfit came cantering across the yard and rode out behind Kennedy. All were heavily armed. When Kennedy had disappeared along the trail to town, Jane hurried across to the corral. She saddled her horse and rode out, intending to head for town in an attempt to get there before her father. But she did not expect him to make it into Squaw Creek, and stayed on his back trail to follow from a safe distance.

They were about halfway to town when Jane saw her father rein in and snatch his Winchester from its saddle boot. Kennedy was sitting atop a crest and Jane could not see beyond his position. The six cowpunchers reined in below the crest and drew their weapons although they could see nothing. Jane pulled in to cover behind them. She saw her father lift his rifle into the aim and fire several shots in quick succession at a target beyond her view. The flat crack of the Winchester flung a string of sullen echoes across the range: immediately several pistols boomed and Kennedy ducked and swung his horse back off the skyline. He and his gun hands rode hard to the right.

Jane retreated deeper into nearby cover. When she looked at her father again he was riding hell for leather away to the right, hunched in his saddle, his gunnies in a tight knot to his immediate rear. Then Jane saw riders appearing on the crest her father had vacated, and she recognized Cole Paston in the lead. Cole looked around, then spurred his horse and gave chase after the fleeing riders. Eight posse men accompanied Cole, and their pistols smoked and flamed as they took up the pursuit. Gun echoes blasted through the silence, rolling like thunder in the distance. The BK crew returned fire immediately.

Buck Kennedy disappeared over a crest to the east. His rifle began firing rapidly from cover. A posse man threw up his arms and vacated his saddle in a nerveless heap, bouncing twice on the hard ground before rolling lifelessly to a halt. Jane sighed heavily and shook her head, unable to see how her father could get out of this particular situation. He was fighting the law, and the odds were long against him. She kicked her horse forward and rode behind the posse, wondering how she could help her father without becoming involved with the law.

The pursuit continued for several miles, the countryside aiding Kennedy and his BK riders, for they ducked into cover each time the posse fired at them and returned fire, compelling the law party to drop back out of range. Then they reached a stretch of fairly level range, and Cole drew his carbine and fired a stream of shots. One of them hit Kennedy's chestnut. The animal faltered, and then went down in a threshing heap. Kennedy managed to kick his feet free of his stirrups. He dived sideways out of the saddle as the horse hit the ground, and rolled away from the cartwheeling animal to finish up in a crumpled heap. He remained motionless.

The gunmen turned at bay and pistol smoke spread rapidly, the shots sounding like pop-guns in the limitless space of the range. The posse surged forward with flaming guns and men fell from their saddles as the fight developed. Cole remained in the lead, trading shot for shot with the gunnies. Jane rode into cover and crouched, listening intently to the ragged affray.

Cole did not hesitate as slugs hammered around him. His teeth were clenched determinedly, and he snapped shots at targets as he rode closer to where Buck Kennedy was lying, backed up by the posse. Gun men vacated their saddles and remained motionless on the grass. A posse man reared up with a bullet in his throat; pitched sideways with blood pumping from his wound, and threshed violently before relaxing in death. Cole swung his Colt as a gunman drew a bead on him. He crooked his trigger finger; the gun blasted, sending a heavy slug into the man's chest. Then there were only two gunmen left in their saddles, and they quickly tossed down their guns and raised their hands in token of surrender. Jane had watched in horror as the fight developed, fearing the worst as she gazed at her father's motionless body.

Cole Paston dismounted to check Kennedy, who was conscious, and two of the posse men dismounted to thrust the rancher into a saddle. The surviving gunmen were handcuffed and helped to mount. The posse swung their horses and rode away towards Squaw Creek, leaving scattered bodies on the hard-baked ground.

147

Jane remained in cover until the riders had gone: they were moving slowly with their prisoners. She circled them, remaining in cover, and rode fast towards the distant town, uncertain how she could help her father. But she was aware that the situation could not be left as it was. Floyd had to be released from jail. She turned over several possibilities in her mind, and with the posse occupied with getting her father back to town, she sensed that the way was clear for her to make an attempt to turn Floyd loose. But she was badly worried as she rode into Squaw Creek.

The town was peaceful, baking in the hot afternoon sun. Jane reined in at the end of the street opposite the livery barn and looked around, her gaze flitting from building to building for as far as she could see. There was little activity at this time of the afternoon. She saw a man seated on a chair outside the entrance to the hotel, and recognized Mart Paston, apparently taking his ease. She rode to the back lots behind the jail and tethered her mount.

Jane was aware that she had very little time to do anything constructive, because when the posse got back her own movements would be severely restricted. She studied the rear of the jail. There was a back door, but it was securely locked and resisted her attempts to open it. She entered the alley beside the jail and walked to the street end, pausing in its shelter and risking a look around. The main street was quiet. She glanced at the front of the hotel and was relieved to see that Mart Paston was no longer seated there.

Acting on an impulse, she went to the front door of the law office, which was ajar, and entered. She paused when she saw Will Eldon seated at the desk. He was scanning a mail-order catalogue. Eldon looked up and smiled, then threw down the catalogue and got to his feet.

'Howdy, Jane,' he greeted. 'Come to see Floyd, huh?'

'If I can,' she replied.

'Well, I'm sorry, but I can't let anyone see him – Cole's orders. He's running things around here now the sheriff is out of action. And Cole left me in charge here. He's gone out to your place to arrest your father. It looks like Buck got himself into a whole lot of trouble yesterday.'

'I'm wondering if there's anything Floyd needs,' Jane said. 'As I am his sister it wouldn't hurt to let me see him for a moment.'

Eldon shook his head. 'I'd get hell from Cole if I went against his orders.'

Jane glanced around the office. She saw a gunbelt containing a holstered pistol hanging from a nail in the back wall behind the desk, and caught her breath as desperation flared through her breast. She looked at Eldon's face. He was smiling.

'You could ask Floyd if there's anything I can get him from the store,' she suggested. 'That wouldn't be against Cole's orders, would it?'

'No, I could do that. Why don't you sit down while I talk to Floyd?'

'Thanks.' Jane slid on to the chair Eldon had vacated. She saw a bunch of keys lying on a corner of the desk. 'Are they the cell keys?' she queried.

'They sure are! I'm not allowed to have them on me when I attend to the prisoners in case they make a grab for

149

them. You just wait here and I'll go talk to Floyd.'

Jane nodded. Eldon took the bunch of keys, selected one from the bunch, and unlocked the door that gave access to the cell block. He left the door open with the keys hanging from the lock. As soon as he disappeared into the cells, Jane snatched the pistol out of the holster behind her. She checked the weapon; it was fully loaded. She jumped up, her heart pounding with mingled excitement and desperation, and hastened into the cell block. The heavy Colt pistol was comfortable in her hand. She paused at the door to take the bunch of keys with her.

Eldon had begun to talk to Floyd Kennedy when he heard Jane at his back. He glanced over his shoulder, his eyes widening at the sight of the pistol in her hand. He dropped a hand to his gun butt, then thought better of it and halted the movement.

'Say, you ain't gonna do anything stupid, are you, Jane?' Eldon demanded. 'Put that gun down before someone gets hurt.'

'You'll get hurt if you don't do like I tell you,' Jane replied. 'I'm taking Floyd out of here, and we'll lock you in, so step aside and don't make a nuisance of yourself.'

'There'll be hell to pay over this,' Eldon said, his teeth clenched. 'Don't do it, Jane. Cole will put you behind bars if you go through with this.'

'Quit stalling and open the damn cell,' Floyd snarled, getting off his bunk. He grabbed the bars of the door and shook it furiously. 'Throw the keys in here, Jane, and I'll undo the door.'

Jane tossed the bunch of keys to Floyd, who stuck a hand between the bars, caught the keys, and unlocked the door. Eldon stuck up his hands. Floyd emerged from the cell, snatched the pistol from Eldon's holster, checked it, then slammed the barrel against the side of Eldon's head. Eldon shifted his hands to protect his skull from another blow, but Floyd seemed to become crazed then and struck Eldon several times, the dull thuds of the gun sounding like a butcher's cleaver hacking at a side of beef. Eldon slumped to the floor. Jane sprang forward and grasped Floyd's gun arm as he aimed the gun at Eldon, seemingly intent on shooting the man.

'Don't shoot him!' Jane gasped. 'For God's sake use your sense Floyd! A shot will bring half the men in town running. You need to get out of here quietly. Cole Paston is out with a posse. I saw them arrest Pa, who was shot last night, and they're bringing him into town. They'll be here in about thirty minutes.'

'Who shot Pa?' Floyd demanded, turning to unlock the adjoining cell. 'Come on out, Lockton,' he ordered the man inside.' We've got work to do.'

Al Lockton, the surviving man of the pair who had beaten up the sheriff in Brady's bar, came out of the cell almost at a run. He skirted Jane and hastened into the front office. Floyd grasped Eldon's collar and dragged him into a cell, left him lying on the floor, and locked the door. He went into the office with Jane following closely. Lockton was buckling a gunbelt around his waist. A pistol was lying on a shelf beside a gun rack; he picked it up and checked it, then slid it into the holster of the gunbelt.

'We'd better make ourselves scarce before that posse gets back,' Lockton said. 'Let's make tracks.'

'The hell we will!' Floyd rasped. 'We're waiting here for

151

the posse to show up, and we'll get the drop on them when they walk in from the street. I want my pa free. Then I've got some old scores to settle around here.'

'I want to settle with that guy who killed Riley.' Lockton grinned. 'Then we better finish off the sheriff. They've got him over at the doc's house, huh?'

'All in good time,' Floyd replied.

'When I reached the end of the street on my way in I saw Mart Paston sitting on a chair in front of the hotel,' Jane said. 'I didn't let him see me, and when I checked the street from the alley mouth beside this office he had gone.'

'I'll drop on to him later,' Floyd said. 'I've waited three years to draw a bead on him. There's gonna be a lot of changes around here now. Let's get ready to face the posse when it rides in. Lockton, cross over the street and wait in the alley opposite. Let the posse start coming into the office before you shoot at them, and watch where you put your slugs – my pa will be right in among them.'

Lockton nodded and grinned. He took a Winchester from a gun rack, checked the mechanism, and then looked in a cupboard for spare shells. He filled his pockets with 44.40 cartridges and left the office. Floyd went to the door and watched Lockton cross the street. There was no sign of the posse yet. He glanced at his sister.

'You'd better get out of here before the shooting starts,' he said.

'No.' Jane shook her head. 'I'm staying. The posse is bringing in Pa and two of the BK gunnies. If you're not careful, Pa will get killed in a shoot-out. Let them come in to the office and then get the drop on them without shooting. You can't fight the whole town, Floyd, so use your sense.'

'You talk too much,' Floyd growled.

'And you're not thinking straight,' Jane retorted.

'Just sit down at that desk and keep out of the way.' Floyd began to pace the office between the desk and the street door. Jane sat down, leaned her elbows on the desk, and lowered her face into her hands.

Cole was relieved when he sighted Squaw Creek. The cow town was drab in the high sun. He glanced sideways at Buck Kennedy, who was slumped in his saddle, the hand-cuffs on his wrists gleaming in the sunlight. The posse entered the street and headed towards the law office. Charlie Swain was riding on the other side of Kennedy, and he grinned when he caught Cole's eye.

'It looks like we did all right, huh?' Swain demanded. 'With Buck behind bars the trouble is over.'

'It won't be over until Floyd is dead,' Cole responded. 'He's full of poison, and if I know him he won't quit until he's got six feet of earth on his chest.'

'But we got him behind bars,' Swain protested. He glanced ahead along the street. 'Say, ain't that Mart sitting in front of the saloon?'

Cole raised a hand to shield his eyes. 'Yeah, it sure is! And that's a beer in his hand.'

'I reckon he has the right idea, don't you?' Swain grinned. 'I'll know what to do when we've put Kennedy in a cell.'

Cole reined up in front of the hotel and eased his weight in the saddle. Mart leaned back in his seat and grinned. He had a rifle propped against the right side of

153

his chair.

'Glad to see you back, Cole,' he said, 'and you got your man. He ain't looking so tough with them bracelets around his wrists, huh? Maybe we can get back to normal now.'

'I can't wait to get me a glass of that beer,' Swain said. 'I'll put Kennedy in a cell if you wanta talk to Mart, Cole.'

Cole glanced around the street. The town was drowsing in the heat of the afternoon sun.

'Go ahead,' he told Swain. 'Leave a couple of the boys in the law office and come on back here for a drink. You deserve it. I'll put some money behind the bar for the rest of the posse. They can drink up later.'

Swain grinned and took hold of Kennedy's reins. He led the BK rancher along the street to the jail. Cole swung down from his saddle and stepped up to the boardwalk. He removed his Stetson, cuffed sweat from his forehead, then slapped at his clothes with his hat, beating out a cloud of dust. Mart held out his half-glass of beer.

'You look like you need this more than I do,' he remarked.

'I sure do.' Cole took the glass and raised it to his lips. He gulped the beer and smacked his lips. 'How are you feeling, Mart? You looked mighty bad when you found me in Liffen's house.'

'I've rested some, but I ain't taking any chances with the Kennedys around, in jail or not.' He reached out and patted his rifle.

Cole put the empty glass on the windowsill behind Mart's head. Mart was smiling. Cole opened his mouth to speak but a burst of gunfire blasted out the silence and

154

strident echoes fled across the town.

'What the hell!' Cole swung to face the direction of the sound. He saw the posse bunched in front of the law office. Gun smoke was flaring from the mouth of the alley opposite the jail. Charlie Swain was falling from his saddle, obviously hit, and Cole spotted a grim figure with a levelled rifle standing in the alley mouth, shooting into the thick of the mounted posse men.

Cole snatched up Mart's rifle, jacked a shell into the breech, and lifted the long gun to his shoulder. He had a clear view of the man in the alley mouth and peered through the sights. He fired two shots, and had the satisfaction of seeing the man spin around before falling against a corner of the alley and then diving into cover.

Mart got stiffly on his feet, favouring his left side. He took his rifle from Cole, who drew his Colt and went at a run along the boardwalk, although the shooting seemed to be over. Gun echoes were fading. Buck Kennedy was pulled out of his saddle by a posse man and thrust towards the law office door. A horse was down in the street, its legs threshing. Charlie Swain was lying motionless on his face in the dust. Cole saw the law office door swing open and Floyd Kennedy stepped into the doorway. Cole gasped in shock. What was Floyd doing out of his cell?

Floyd shot the posse man holding his father, grabbed Buck Kennedy, and pulled him into the office. The door was slammed. It had happened so quickly that the surviving posse men had no chance to react. Four of them – all that was left of the posse – ran for cover. Cole dashed along the street, his pistol ready. He saw one of the wooden shutters that Charlie Swain had nailed up in place of the shattered law office window suddenly fall outwards as it was hammered loose from inside. He ducked to one side when a burst of shooting sprayed deadly slugs around the street.

'Come and get it!' Floyd Kennedy shouted. 'Send Mart Paston out front and I'll finish him first.'

Cole sent two shots into the front of the law office, aiming for a lower corner where gun smoke was drifting. He dropped to one knee as a slug came back at him, snarling in his left ear. One of the posse men shouted a high-pitched warning, and Cole turned his head to see a figure in the alley opposite in the act of lifting a pistol into the aim. It was Lockton, who had shot Charlie Swain. He had blood on his shirtfront and his gun wavered in his hand, but he was not out of the fight. Cole triggered a shot, saw Lockton jerk, and swung back to cover the front of the law office as the man went down on his face.

Mart came up, limping badly, his rifle in his right hand, his face set in an expression of grim eagerness. Cole covered the front of the office. There was no sign of Floyd now, but he could hear Floyd's voice raging at someone inside the office – probably Buck Kennedy.

'Hey, Floyd,' Cole yelled, 'if you've got any sense you'll throw out your gun and give up. The place is surrounded, front and back. You can't get away. Don't make this any worse than it has to be.'

'Go to hell!' Floyd yelled, and two shots hammered. Dust flicked up near Cole's right boot.

Cole replied instantly, driving two shots into the bottom right-hand corner of the space left by the discarded shutter. Mart took the opportunity of dodging into the alley to the left of the office, and then eased out again, his rifle ready for action. He fired three shots into the office. Cole ran forward and pressed his back against the front wall of the office to the right of the spot where Floyd was crouching inside.

'We've got you dead to rights, Floyd,' Cole called. 'Do something right for a change and call it off. You can't win nohow!'

Mart eased closer to the window space, the butt of his Winchester in his shoulder, his finger tight against the trigger. He fired quickly, sending two more shots into the office, and then dashed forward to thrust the rifle muzzle into the office and fired again.

'OK, Cole,' Mart said, without taking his eyes from the interior of the office. 'I got Floyd. Kick in the door while I cover Buck. It's all over.'

Cole attacked the door of the office, and lunged inside as woodwork splintered. He found Floyd stretched out on the floor just inside. Buck Kennedy was standing over by the desk, where Jane Kennedy sat, her face in her hands. Gunsmoke was swirling around them.

Cole holstered his gun. Relief swilled through him. He bent to check Floyd, who was dead, and then went to grasp Buck Kennedy's arm. He led the rancher into the cell block, where Will Edlon was standing tensely at the door of the cell in which he had been locked. The cell keys were lying on the floor to one side. Cole picked them up, freed Eldon, and pushed Buck Kennedy into his place.

Eldon started a gabbled explanation of what had happened but Cole cut him short.

'Not now, Will,' he said. 'Leave it till later.'

Cole had too much to think about right now. He knew

enough about what had happened in the past to be able to piece it all together, given time. Buck Kennedy would probably keep his mouth shut, but the sheriff would talk, and then it would all come out. He sighed and went back into the front office, his mouth dry, his nostrils filled with gunsmoke, and relief swelling in his mind.